A HOLIDAY ROM-COM

ELFED UP
~ THIS ~
CHRISTMAS

BY

LAUREN BAKER

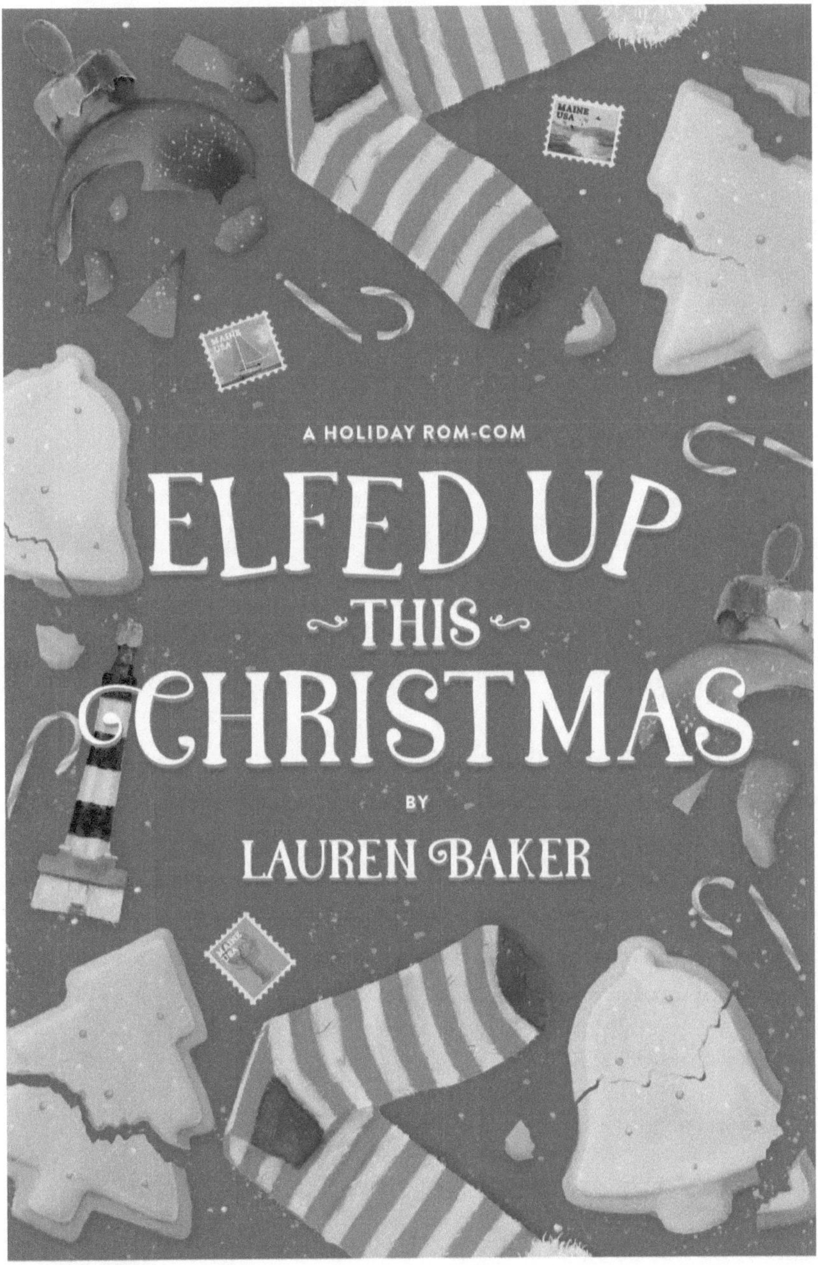

First Edition: September 26, 2025

Book Cover by Shelby Schena

Book Design by Tea and Tales Publishing LLC

ISBN: 979-8-9988436-3-1

Contents

Dedication   1

1. Coffee & Chaos   3

2. One Elf, Two...   18

3. Expectations A'Plenty   33

4. Cinnamon Rolls & Slip of Tongues   41

5. Photoshoots & Contempt   52

6. Hot & Cold   58

7. Friendly Interference   63

8. Late Night Baking   68

9. One Wall Down   76

10. Banquet Bombshell   83

11. Speeches Turned Spoiled   91

12. Merry Mistep   103

13. Ho, Ho, Help!   109

14. Mistakes and Mischief   116

15. Hark the Festival   128

16. Alleyways Best Kept Secret   140

17. Throwing Shade (& Snow)   158

18. Dinner & A Show   170

19. Sister Showdown   181

20. Yuletide Waltz   192

21. When the Music Fades   208

22. No Magic Needed, Just Hearts   216

23. A Recipe to Forever   227

To anyone dealing with grief this holiday season—may you find a little sparkle, a little laughter, and a little magic within these pages!

1

Coffee & Chaos

Ginger

"Okay, Ginger, you got this."

If I ever thought my arch-nemesis would be an espresso machine, I would've never taken this assignment.

For the 5th time in a row, the espresso wasn't pouring correctly into the cup and began squirting out hot, scalding streams. Forcing me to once again, use my oven mitt for protection before turning it off. Sighing, I move the red curl from my face; the same infuriating curl that never stayed put no matter how much foam setter I use.

"This is ridiculous. Do they not try to set us up somewhere believable? I mean, the baking portion I can handle. But this! This...dastardly machine is going to ruin everything!"

I absent-mindedly hit the side of the machine, immediately regretting it as my hand stung from impact of flesh to metal.

Smooth. Now you're going to be injured before you even get customers.

As it turned out, being a barista at a small coffee shop in the middle of Maine was harder than I thought. When I first accepted this job, I would've sworn it didn't involve dealing with an off-the-fritz coffee machine from Hell. Or maybe I skipped over that part in the job description. If my posting here was going to work, I needed to figure this out ASAP.

I took the manual for the evil device in my hand and tried to see what I was doing so wrong. Flipping to the page with the instructions for the espresso portion; I read the instructions out loud.

"Please make sure there is no obstruction in the portafilter. Tamp down coffee grounds lightly before insertion."

"Ah ha! I see.."

Doing as the instructions stated, I placed the part back in place and watched in awe, as *finally,* it poured beautiful, smooth espresso into the to-go cup I was using for practice. The smell of coffee filled the air, and I did a little wiggle dance at my own cleverness for figuring it out.

Or you should have read the instructions from the start and you wouldn't have spent the last half an hour fighting a coffee machine.

I finished up my vanilla latte by steaming the milk, which surprisingly wasn't as hard, since this was one of those fancy machines that steamed it for you after placing the wand inside the cup.

The wonders of technology! We gotta get one of these at the North Pole! Would spruce up coffee breaks.

Taking a sip of my hard-won coffee, I took some deep breaths and looked around the café. It was quaint, but incredibly cute. With large windows overlooking the town square, it had a collection of booths and tables strewn about in a haphazard way. The bakery display case sat beneath the coffee station, filled with Christmas themed cookies, sweet treats and quiches–the perfect combination for a little snack on a cold winter's day! I decided to make a mental note for myself when I opened later that afternoon, to use a little of my magic to add some Christmas bows and decorations, to make the ambiance more inviting.

Finishing off the last of my coffee, I pulled the letter containing my work assignment from the back pocket of my jeans–which by the way, was way more comfortable than I'd ever imagined! Why didn't we wear these at the Pole? Maybe I should put that in the suggestion box at HR.

The letter was embossed with a large swirling *SC & Co.* on the envelope which glimmered in sparkly red ink. I always thought it made us sound like a big business corporation being called *Santa Claus & Company*–but I guess we sort of were! My department was in charge of Christmas Spirit, and we were often referred to as Santa's Helpers; although I suggested the Holly Jolly Fun Squad last year at the end of year group retreat, (we went to Hawaii; I never want to be so sunburned again, please and thank you,) and got zero votes despite how cute it sounded.

Our division was in charge of creating more Christmas Spirit in the world. In hard times throughout history, we have been transplanted all over in towns who are needing help with cultivating Christmas joy, cheer, love, good will to neighbors, giving to those in need, or even help with individuals who have had a particularly tough time in life and need some holiday Spirit to lift them up or help them out of a rut.

Every year, Elves were sent to the places in desperate need of cheer, in hopes that with a little magic, we could bring people closer together and raise morale before the very important holiday. The Christmas Spirit around the world is an essential power source for the North Pole—without it, there would be no toys, gifts, or holiday fun. Christmas itself would cease to exist.

It is a very important job to be assigned, and I was lucky to finally be given my first post! I was *not* going to mess this up. If I succeeded in raising the Spirit levels here, I could get promoted! Or become one of the top Elves in the department. However, being one of Santa's Helpers wasn't what I hoped to do with my life.

My true dream was to be transferred to the bakery department—and the most elite bakery in the world was located right in the North Pole. Many didn't know, but we baked and transported hundreds of thousands of goodies a year to shops all the way from Paris to Alaska. To be a baker there is one of the top tiers in the Pole, it is a position coveted even higher than toy makers. The craftsmanship of the pastries, cookies and chocolate sculptures—you heard me, they make masterpieces out of chocolate—was truly something no other bakery could compare to in the world.

But rarely in the Pole was there transfer between departments. Typically, it was a family run affair. My family has been Santa's Helpers since the beginning of Christmas. My great-great-great-great grandmother was the first in our lineage to be posted in a town in Holland to spread the cheer. The legend of how she saved the town from a neighboring village who wanted to cut down all the forest nearby—while my grandmother rallied the townsfolk and convinced them that the trees should be used for something, and not completely destroyed; is a tale we still speak of in our household—gathered around the tree each Christmas Eve night. By showing the town the advantage of turning it into a thriving Christmas tree farm, while also promoting sustainability by replanting new forests each year, it was a giant success.

My great-grandmother was the first Elf to stop a "commercializing" entity, and begin the first Christmas tree farm that saved the town financially, *and* raised Christmas Spirit to record-breaking levels. Granted, this was back 200 years ago, so conglomerate companies didn't quite exist yet, so you can see why she was a total badass.

Anyways, typically you followed the profession your family lineage upheld. Children of toy makers built toys. Children of reindeer keepers handled and cared for the reindeer. So on and so forth...

But even at a young age, I felt like baking was in my blood. I knew it was the passion I was called to. I could whip up hundreds of perfectly decorated cookies, make you dozens of the most delicious pies, and even create miniature chocolate sculptures I practiced in secret in hopes of one day developing my skills further. My miniature chocolate skiing polar bear won the amateur chocolate sculpture contest 2 years ago—granted, I had to go under an alias name as I wasn't technically allowed to enter. I was a Helper, I wasn't supposed to be crafting chocolate creations.

It is a sad reality of the Pole. Although I adore my home, the old tradition of becoming whatever your family had been, is not only outdated, but disheartening. I mean, come on, not every toy maker is automatically perfect at building toys. One of them has to be bad at it, right?

This conversation was never something I could bring up; it was too taboo to want to be in any other department. But baking made me feel creative and alive. Being able to bring something to life that starts out as a mere ball of dough, is art to me. At least part of the deal during this mission is that I can bake, as the café needs treats for its customers to enjoy. It is a welcomed challenge.

Unfolding the letter, I re-read the town details of where I'd be staying for the next month. Having arrived a few days after Thanksgiving to have some time to spark up this town before Christmas!

Everly Cove is a quiet fishing town nestled on the coast of Maine. It once blossomed as a must-see spot for Christmas festivities and dazzling decorations. People would travel from all across the country to see the lights and parade, always deemed as one of the top spots in the United States to visit for the holiday season. But 5 years ago, it went from a picturesque Hallmark movie extravaganza–to ghost town. *Everything stopped.*

The first year we heard the news of this abrupt change, a group of tourists flooded the once 'Decked-out-in-holly' town when they realized: there were no decorations. The town was a wasteland. When the visitors asked a small bookshop owner why there were no lights or shows, the old man stated that, "Over celebratory shenanigans during Christmas was banned, henceforth." Actually, it was the presiding mayor who made this absurd statement. Nobody truly knew what happened. Ever since, there hasn't been a single twinkle light in sight.

As one can see, there is a severe issue at hand. Yes, there are lots of places that go all out for the holidays, but this town was special. It brought people from all walks of life, it showed what tremendous things can happen when people work together, and it was one of the places we got such an ample amount of our energy from. To lose it, not only as an energy source, but as a place of camaraderie and phenomenal Spirit that ushered in the greatest time of the year, was a travesty.

But I was going to do something about it!

For years, a Helper was sent to investigate the falling out of the town, but everybody came back empty-handed. It has become the ultimate mystery back at Headquarters. A mystery I was determined to solve.

*Not that any other agent was ever able to...not like they sent Helpers who have been doing this job for centuries, and **they** still couldn't fix it..*

But I'm Ginger! That's part of my plan: charm (or annoy, depending on who you ask) the pants off of people until I get my way! That's how it worked with this promotion, even if my coworkers said it was only because they were desperate to send someone just for formality's sake–it didn't matter. I was too stubborn to give up, challenges being my specialty. When the inter-departmental reindeer crisis a few years back occurred and the reindeer all decided to walk off the job–you heard me–I was the one who stepped up to mediate!

I rushed to speak with the head reindeer, which, no–it is not Rudolph. He retired years ago and is now living happily with his family on a large plot of wooded area outside Santa's Village. This reindeer's name was Captain, and he was as ruthless an adversary as any villain in an action movie! They became incessantly irritated by their lack of time off and inadequate quarter arrangements.

But after a long sit down with him, we came to an agreement: 2 weeks off for vacation leave and 5 sick days for all reindeer. Not to mention, they now have more comfortable accommodations including memory foam beds, fresh hay whenever they wish, and even a reindeer snack dispenser! (Don't tell anyone this, but that dispenser does have the best carrots in all the village. I sneak a few now and again...They make the most delicious vegetable soup!) Now, Captain will only speak with me when it comes to their needs. We have become good friends, and he ended up not being as frightening as I thought. We typically have afternoon cake together on Thursdays, and catch up on the past week's gossip.

Yes, I should've mentioned; I speak to animals. The only Elf known to do so! You think they'd be impressed, but I guess when you can relay pretty much anything from furry friends–it's not as interesting a gift as one might think. When I was little, all the kids thought it was the coolest thing ever. They would often bring their pets from home and ask me what they thought about them as owners; you can imagine how that went...After one incident where the pet arctic fox that belonged to a boy named Rufus said he'd rather be taken by a pack of wolves than stay with him any longer, and I relayed that rude message—people didn't think my 'gift' was quite so interesting anymore.

When I came home crying, asking my parents why I was the only one able to do this, they couldn't answer. We scanned dozens of family documents, seeing if anyone before mentioned being able to speak to animals. I spent hours in the North Pole archives to find out if any other Elves were recorded to have the same ability, but in the end, there was nothing about it other than me.

Once the hype of my talents died down, I took it as another sign that I'm just the weird Elf on the block. But it's been fun, and helpful throughout my life! You wouldn't believe the things I have heard through the years.

My best friend is my cat Gimli, who is the snarkiest creature to walk this planet. He does what he wants, how he pleases, and the word "no" doesn't live in his vocabulary. He's spoiled rotten, but he's also been the greatest companion I've ever known. He doesn't play, or chase critters, or even do much other than sleep and judge me sideways from across the room; but he's my little familiar and I don't go anywhere without him.

The black and white, chunky furball was currently cleaning his paws on a stool nearby. Most cafés don't allow pets, but one of the bonuses about this gig is that I can change the café as I see fit, and I plan to fit, "Bring your friendly pets for lattes," into the policies. That way, it won't be odd that Gimli is around all the time. I did tell him that if he stepped one paw in the actual kitchen though, he'd better hope I don't make Cat Brûlée a signature item on the menu.

I'd already put a sign out front saying pets were welcome, and I may have *magically* cooked up some dog and cat treats to put on display as well. So far, things were going great. The bakery portion was set; I planned myself for 6 new specialties per week to showcase (all of which I only needed to bake one and then my magic would duplicate as many as needed,) and with the coffee machine figured out–I could turn my attentions to what I actually came here for: To find out *how* and *why* this adorable Christmas town fell off the map, and how could we get it back to its former glory again.

My cover was in motion, as a friendly neighborhood barista oozing with charm, was bound to loosen enough lips to let me in on what was really going on here. If I could integrate myself, I could use my magic and cunning to come up with a game plan to restore the Christmas Spirit once and for all.

People love telling their lives to cute baristas, right? It's like a dentist or a barber; they don't even realize they're doing it!

I walked to the front windows, the blinds down temporarily to keep out prying eyes until the opening this afternoon. With a wave of my hand, a large winter bouquet appeared in my arms, and I set it down on the ledge beneath the window, one for either side of the door. A rather insolent meow echoed across the room towards me. Turning with my hands on my hips, I glare at Gimli.

"It's definitely NOT too much, sir. My decorations are lovely and inviting. You are just a cranky cat with nothing better to do but mock me. If you are so much better, what would you do instead?"

Gimli responded with a bored yowl, jumping off the stool he'd perched upon, and strolled leisurely in my direction.

"No, a cat shaped sculpture in the likeness of you, strung with Christmas lights, is worse. Not better. Don't nag me either, I need to run some errands before the opening. If you're bored, you're free to walk your tail back to the cottage and take a nap or something. You remember how to get there, right?"

Gimli mewed in response, which was his version of a yes, and I opened the door. The tinkling bell above it went off as I watched him scamper across the courtyard that was the town square, and down the back alley of the tailor's shop across the street, only a few blocks away from the cozy cottage we were staying in for the time being. Gimli was quite independent, he often explored places and went out on his own, so he'd be far more comfortable at the cottage than sitting around here all day.

Plus, I needed to go to the bank to get some cash for the cash register at the café for the opening and drop a letter to HQ at the post office. Luckily, both were a few minutes walk from here. I read it on the pamphlet "Things to Do and See in the Town of Everly Cove," I swiped off the small table at the coffee shop displaying local businesses' information, featuring a town map. Inside the pamphlet was also a restaurant in town called "Everly's Best." I know I could whip something up myself–but what better way to get to know the locals than to eat locally?

I'd set up an interview for my first ever employee to meet me at the café after I'd done my errands, in hopes to get to know them before the big grand re-opening of the shop. Apparently her name was Izabelle, and she'd been picked by the agency for me before I arrived. She'd sort of manage the café for me whenever I needed, had excellent skills and references, and wasn't prone to skipping out on work whenever she felt like it. It was exactly who I needed to help keep the café afloat while I also ran around finagling connections, gathering information, and getting to know the locals, to find the solution to our greatly increasing problem.

Grabbing my coat, I threw it on and pulled my fuzzy ear muffs out from one of the pockets. Placing them on my head, making sure to avoid the hard worked ringlets I did that morning or the hair set in two small buns atop of my head, I walked out the front door and locked it. I looked up at the new coffee shop sign name, and smiled to myself. This, too, was a perk of the job; I got to name the café whatever I wished: ***Tinsel Brews & Sweets***, after my namesake, in swirling green lettering. You heard right, Ginger Tinsel finally put her name on something!

Turning around, knowing a ridiculous smile was taking over, I took in the quaint square before me. All in all, it was the cutest town I've ever seen! Made entirely out of brick and cobblestone, the sidewalks were lined with green wrought-iron benches, throughout the square old arc lamps brought a hint of the past in with the present, and right dab in the center was a large opening where an old clock tower stood proudly. With the light flurry beginning to pick up, it was absolutely beautiful.

But it was also eerily quiet. We were only a few weeks away from Christmas and there wasn't a soul around. No merry families shopping for gifts, no tourists snapping shots of the charming scene, and no vendors on the street handing out blazing hot cocoa while strolling locals enjoyed the fresh snow.

What happened here?

My assignment here came with a folder (which was now laying willy-nilly across the bed back at the cottage) and with it, came photos and descriptions of what Everly Cove used to be like during Christmastime. I remember specifically picking up a photo with the town decorated from top to bottom with string lights, wreaths, bows, and even ice sculptures! The town square was filled to the brim with people enjoying festivities such as knap-sack racing, pin the carrot on the snowman, miniature ice-sculpture contests, pie contests, caroling, carriage rides, and so much more. It was absolutely the place to visit during the holidays, and it was sad to see how it was now; empty and lonely.

Not for long! Before they know it, they'll be laughing and caroling to their heart's content again in this square. They won't know what ginger-haired Elf hit them!

I tightened my ear muffs and crunched my way through the snow building up on the sidewalk. Cold air brushed my cheeks and snowflakes were landing on my eyelashes. Chuckling, I blinked them away and crossed the street towards the bank. Once there, I got the usual currency for the café (The Pole uses coins that are different from these but I studied them thoroughly before arriving here) and strode on to the post office.

This was definitely not your typical post office, though. It was a small wooden building wedged between the local attorney's office and a shop for trinkets and gifts, both of which were brick—so this office was only made cuter by the sheer fact it didn't seem to belong; like someone picked it up from somewhere else and squeezed it with all their might into this gap between the two others. Shaded in baby-blue, it had an itty-bitty front porch covered by an awning. An outgoing mailbox sat prominently in the corner of the porch, and a propped-up sign read "Open!" beside the front door.

Pushing the door open, I was greeted by a blast of warm air, wriggling my nose from the abrupt temperature change; it was, however, a warm welcome. In front of me was a counter, a rack off to the left with various sized envelopes and a few boxes, and another counter displaying stamps. On the far right wall was an enlarged photo of what looked to be a Saint Bernard dog holding a letter in his mouth. Beneath said picture, was who I was assuming was the infamous hound himself. An actual, large Saint Bernard laid in a dog bed beneath the picture, a homemade sign nailed behind him on the wall reading "Zeus' Throne." Thankfully, it didn't seem I would be the only person bringing their pet to work with them—and this one seemed as obsessed with their pet as I was.

That might work out to my advantage...a way in!

Zeus raised his head as I passed, yawned, and casually stood up, stretching himself. I walked to the large counter and found a bell. Ringing it, I waited for someone to come. Zeus walked to me and I put a hand out, waiting to see if he'd find a scratch from me pleasant; one animal lover to another knows you never pet one without its permission. He sniffed it and leaned his large, soft head in; I got the okay.

Leaning lower, I whispered to ask his favorite scratching spot. Zeus let out a happy bark, letting me know it was right behind the ears he adored most. I went to work giving the good boy a big ol' scratch, while he wagged his tail and panted. One back foot rose up to do that thing dogs do when a scratch is too good. I laughed and patted him once on the head before rising back up to look behind the counter. No one had come yet.

I proceeded to ring the bell again...silence. Then the door behind me opened and startled me. I looked around to see a man walking up to the counter. He stood a good bit taller than me as he approached, but that wasn't hard to do. Elf remember? With brown skin that made it look like he'd been on vacation in the tropics rather than the frosty cold of Maine, short, curly black hair, and square framed glasses, like a disheveled professor-type. He wore a large coat that reached the top of his knees and a maroon and navy scarf.

Walking towards the counter, he ignored my presence and rang the bell absentmindedly. To occupy the wait, I returned to giving Zeus compliments and more head scratches. When no answer came, just as my experience, he turned to me frustrated.

"You must be the new clerk my aunt hired. If you'd be so kind as to stop your incessant petting of my dog, I'd like to mail a letter quickly."

What?! Who the hell does this guy think he is?

2

One Elf, Two...

Ginger

I gave Zeus one final pat on the head, and he all but rolled his eyes at his apparent owner when I stood to face the incredulous man.

"I apologize for giving the sweet boy love, I had no idea he was your dog considering he's here at the post office. But for your information, I am not the new post office clerk, *sir*. I too, am merely trying to send a letter and no one is answering the bell."

I hoped I filled my words with half as much disdain as the ungentlemanly man did with his rude introduction. He eyed me up and down, disbelief flickering behind his eyes, as if no one dared to stand up to him before or give him a taste of his own medicine. Well, nobody belittled Ginger Tinsel and didn't get a sucker punch of sass–it came with the neatly, multi-colored package.

The man awkwardly adjusted his scarf, unwrapping it slightly to let it fall on either side of his chest. Without making eye contact again, he spoke with an air of superiority rather than one that should've been an apology.

"My aunt must've needed to run an errand. I keep telling her she needs to put the "Be back soon" sign on the front door, but she always forgets. And yes, Zeus is my dog, but I work running around the town most of the day, and he hates staying at my house alone. I drop him off here to be with my aunt so he has company; he enjoys greeting customers. She adores him, and helps with little things during the day. It's a win, win."

Zeus walked around us and stood beside the man, who at last acknowledged him and gave a scratch on his head. Zeus' tail wagged happily and he laid on the floor by the man's feet. I wanted to ask Zeus what he saw in this grumpy guy as his owner, but then I'd end up looking like a crazy person talking to the dog like that. That would not be the first impression I'd want to leave in this town: "Crazy woman running coffee shop talks to animals like they can talk back."

Yeah, no thanks. I'd be run out of this town faster than I could even set roots here. And that was not part of the plan. But coming across the first townsperson and it going this atrociously, was also not going as I intended.

Silence lingered in the post office for several seconds, neither of us wanted to be the next to speak. I wrinkled my nose, trying to quell the irritation I had at the man–who very clearly showed attractiveness and good manners did not go hand in hand. Because, unfortunately, this man was drop-dead *gorgeous*! The way he spoke, a mixture of Northern and something else I couldn't quite place, was tantalizing to say the least. But for all his good looks, he was most certainly a beast. Poor thing. Goes to show that personality didn't always match with handsomeness–this man was cold, shallow, and downright **not** somebody I wished to engage with further.

I readied my armor; it might've been pointless, but something about him itched me the wrong way. He wasn't going to get the last word in, especially if he was determined to be unpleasant–I could be, too.

"Do you often go around accusing strangers in such a way?" I slowly turned to face him, although he did his best to ignore me.

"No, I don't. I've never seen you around here, I only assumed."

I huffed at his response, shifting on my feet uncomfortably, which finally got his attention. He stared his captivating, honey-brown eyes down at me over his glasses.

"I just moved here, I'm the new owner and operator of the coffee shop in the square."

This bit of news grabbed his attention. He folded his arms over his chest, and I had to keep myself from noticing that the fabric of his jacket had a hard time stretching over his defined muscles. Even with layers on, you could tell this man was very...fit.

For Frosty's sake, Ginger. Keep it together!

He raised an eyebrow at me, which elicited a mixed feeling of attraction and absolute frustration; how could one man encapsulate both?

One stranger. You keep forgetting that part, you don't know anything about this man.

When he spoke again, his mocking tone returned, and it made my fists clench inside my coat pocket.

"Another owner of the coffee shop? Really? Seriously, the amount of different people who've come and gone from that place is impressive. You really think you can manage? You don't know this god-forsaken town like I do. People here are picky. If you don't make their cappuccino with light foam just right, they write you off. That's why nobody has been able to keep that place going for longer than a few months. You're definitely taking on quite the challenge Ms..?" His voice trailed off, and I tempered my rising annoyance.

"Ms. Tinsel. And yes.. It hasn't had much success. But I am determined to make it one! I also bake, so I think the townsfolk will come to enjoy my treats soon enough. Now, if you'll excuse me, I'd rather be eaten for dinner by a Yeti, than to be in your *fine* presence any longer. I'll bring my letter back later.."

My patience had reached its end. I was hungry, exhausted from figuring out that dang espresso monster earlier, and I was in no mood to be berated by a stuck-up man—no matter how easy on the eyes he was. Without another word, I turned to pet Zeus a final time. He whimpered in response, sad for my leaving.

"Sorry, boy. Have this, okay?"

From my pocket, I magically pulled out a dog biscuit; one of my own making—a mixture of peanut butter and blueberry; it was always a fan favorite back at the Pole. Zeus took the treat gently from my hand, and sat back on his hind legs wagging his tail, engulfing the treat almost instantly. I smiled at him and did my utmost to not look at the man again as I strolled angrily out of the post office into the chilly air.

Once outside, I covered my mouth with my mittens and let out a small, embittered scream.

"The absolute nerve. I thought small town people were supposed to be nice and welcoming?"

Guess he missed that memo.

I pulled out of my pocket a small device, resembling a normal cellphone, called a Spiritometer. It allowed someone to calculate the amount of Christmas Spirit either in an individual, or a certain area. Right now, the screen flashed a momentary image of red and green ornaments as it turned on. Clicking on it, I saw the details it provided.

Location: Everly Cove, Maine

Time: 11:30 am

Christmas Spirit Scale: -38 %

I sighed and forced the device back into my pocket. Everly Cove has been in the negatives ever since they stopped celebrating Christmas. If I am going to get this place back on track, I am going to have to get to the bottom of this quickly. I found my way drudging through the snow towards the restaurant, Everly's Best.

Apparently, according to the pamphlet I picked up at the café, it wasn't in town at all. Instead, it sat on the rocky shoreline on the outskirts of town, which wasn't ideal since this Elf can't drive a car. Yeah, you heard me. No car. So how was I supposed to get there? I made a meeting there with my single employee in 30 mins! Even though it was only about a 10 minute drive, by the time my car service arrived, I would most definitely be late.

Did every agent who came here end up being unable to get around easily?

With the opening in less than a few hours, there was no way I'd make it back in time to prepare everything. I had a large ribbon to do a ribbon cutting, goody bags with pet treats, candy canes to still put together, and I needed to get Izabelle comfortable enough to take the lead on drink orders.

Time is rapidly running out, and I was too caught up in the excitement of my first case to check the distance to the restaurant. I reached back into my pocket once again for my Spiritometer–which functioned as a cellphone as well–and dialed Izabelle's number the agency gave me. When she finally answered, I was taken by surprise.

"Ginger, hi! I meant to call earlier but I figured you'd be here at the café. I'm here outside waiting for you. I thought it might be better to talk here so I can start right away with any preparations you may have."

I took a deep breath and did a small fist pump. This girl was far smarter than I was in this situation.

Thank everything that is jolly and bright!

"Hi Izabelle! Yes, I am so terribly sorry for my inability to see how far the restaurant was with the opening happening soon. Thank you for coming here! I'm just down the street at the post office, I'll meet you there in a moment. And don't worry, I'll make something good for us to eat for lunch!"

Izabelle chimed in quickly, "No need! I ordered from the restaurant early and brought lunch for us both. See you in a minute!"

Izabelle promptly hung up, and I wondered to myself if I could give that girl a raise already. She could very well be my own personal Rudolf, coming in and saving the day at the café before we even open. I raced back down the streets to the café and saw a blur all in black standing in front of the hazel green door. When I approached, the girl turned and waved at me casually. She sounded way different on the phone than she looked in person.

She wore a slick black coat with a hood lined with black fur. Her raven colored hair trickled down in perfect waves, the ends of which had red highlights in ombre, progressively getting lighter at the tips. She had what had to be salon-skilled winged, purple eyeliner, and a light purple tinted shade of lip gloss stood out against her stark white smile. She was my complete antithesis in looks, but she was quite beautiful in a mysterious "I'll still cut you" type of way. Izabelle strode towards me and reached out a leather, gloved hand, holding a plastic bag filled with to-go containers in the other.

"Ginger, it's nice to finally meet you. I've heard a lot about you."

My voice caught in the back of my throat. "You have?" I didn't know the agency would tell much about who or more specifically, what I am. Would they?

"Yeah, the hiring agency that called me said you were the new bright star of this little town looking for a competent café manager. They mentioned you have some different ideas for how to get this place popular again. If that's the case, I'm excited to be a part of it."

I still felt confused by her choice of words, but I was so thankful to have some help. Although running the café was my cover, I would need time away so I can get an idea of what is happening here.

Otherwise, I'd be making lattes and baguettes with no way to move forward—which is exactly what happened to all my predecessors. That wouldn't happen with me. I needed somebody who could run the shop while I'm out, and still maintain decorum to show I'm becoming an integrated part of the community. Izabelle could very well be the person helping me the most here, I needed to make sure this meeting went well. Otherwise, I'll be hosting a grand opening of the café alone, fumbling a coffee machine that I hardly got working before, with possible patrons looking for perfection—as the attractive, but coarse guy back at the post office mentioned prior.

It is so important I make a good impression with this opening, as it is really my one true ticket into getting a foot in the door with the townsfolk. If this doesn't work out...I might as well be packing my stuff and crawling back home to the embarrassment and disappointment of my entire Santa Helper legendary family. Then, I could kiss my one hope at a possible transfer of departments goodbye.

I returned Izabelle's firm handshake and nodded. "That is exactly what I need! I really hope that you'll be managing enough to keep things running on a day-to-day basis here. I will, of course, continue to provide the baked goods each day, but it would be better to have someone here who knows how to run everything as well other than myself."

"I think that won't be a problem. Should we go inside and discuss further? I brought soup and salads, I hope you don't mind!"

The sudden mention of food made my stomach rumble in response. I couldn't even remember the last time I ate. I got into the town so late the night before and immediately dropped my belongings off at the cottage and rushed to the shop in the morning, I don't know if I ate anything at all.

I smiled at Izabelle gratefully. "That is perfect, thank you for bringing it. Let's get inside out of this cold!"

It was a saying I'd practiced in the mirror several times back at the Pole. Because, Elves don't actually get cold! In fact, it felt blazingly warm here compared to back home. I'd definitely need to change tops before the opening. It feels like I was back on that blasted Hawaii trip again. But when you're used to negative 60s, you find anywhere else to feel like a blazing sun. When agents are being sent anywhere, part of our training requires us to sit in saunas and practice wearing layers of warm clothing so that we can convince everyone else who finds this weather freezing, that we are also cold. Saunas are my least favorite things in the world; maybe I should've considered that when I took that trip to Hawaii...

Fumbling for my keys, I unlocked the door and looked around for my furry familiar. I made sure to put a cat door in the back of the building so he could come in and out as he pleased. Thinking that he would stay at the cottage all day, I was pleasantly surprised to see him curled up on the bench of one of the booth seats, purring contentedly. Seeing him here made me feel immediately calmer. Although he was a pain in the behind more often than not, he was a part of home here with me, and I was starting to miss it already.

Turning on the lights, I picked the small round table in the middle and took my coat off, placing it over the back of the chair. Izabelle did the same, and I couldn't help but admire the tattooed arm sleeve she had under a black laced blouse with puffy sleeves that cut off at the elbow. Her midriff showed and it made me wonder if she ran hot as well. I only hoped as she started unpacking the containers she brought, that I wasn't sweating more than typical for this weather.

We took a moment to take a few bites of our salads before diving in, and I was so happy to be eating, I think I could've eaten the entire thing without saying a single word. But I dabbed my mouth with a napkin and set it aside for the time being.

"So Izabelle, how long have you been managing restaurants?"

Izabelle set her salad aside as well, and leaned back with one arm propped up on the back of the chair. She raised her eyebrow at me, like she was shocked about something.

"You don't know? Ginger, I'm from *SC & Co.* I'm an Elf in the Operations division."

My mouth dropped open. This girl dressed in all black from head to toe, piercings, ripped jeans and the literal polar opposite of anybody I'd seen back home, was an Elf! Most Elves dressed similarly to me, although we didn't have specific uniforms, the colors red, green and white, or the occasional blue tones, were usually preferred amongst every person I knew. Granted, I didn't get out of my own department much and the Pole was said to be bigger than I'd explored. Still, I was dumbfounded. Clearly she noticed and took the liberty to pull her hair behind her *pointed* ears—which were pierced in several places.

"Izabelle, I don't understand. I thought I was the only Elf sent on this mission. Nobody informed me that anyone else would be coming."

Izabelle did her best to not make eye contact. She was visibly uncomfortable.

"Well...it was last minute." She paused, seeming to be thinking of the best way to deliver her next words. "Your sister actually asked me to come."

"You've got to be kidding me."

My sister.

Clara Tinsel was the last person on the planet whose name I wanted to hear right now. Being one of 4 sisters, Clara is the oldest–and most intrusive, annoying, out-of-this world, bigheaded sibling I could've gotten in this life. She was also my superior at the agency. From the time I was old enough to start being a Helper, my sister was there sticking her perfect button nose in every single assignment I had. She seemed to make it her life's mission to sabotage or undermine my every move. My two younger sisters, Bianca and Esme, she doted on like a second mother. There was never a time where she gave that same kindness and nurturing to me–perhaps we were too close in age with Clara being 32, myself at 29, and the twins trailing 4 years behind me.

Ever since we were little, we had a vicious and unending rivalry with each other. Snowball fights were deadly, resulting in near-maiming and frozen digits at the sheer effort we exerted into every one of them. Neither of us would bow out, and it would take my father to come drag us both away, one under each arm, until we were kicking and screaming and blue in the face, to call the battle quits.

The fact was, my sister has been a manager of mine for several years, but this was the first case I was taking all on my own that, up until now, my sister hadn't stuck her nose in.

So much for doing this on my own..

It was only a matter of time for her to involve herself, I don't know why I expected any different. The last case I had, was a small one where I was tasked with being on the call center floor for agents in need of help on missions. The first week was smooth as buttercream icing! I was so proud to have a position of my own, away from my sister, who was one of 3 managers of the main branch who dispatched agents. This job didn't see much action, but we were an essential cog in the machine to assist Helpers in real time. I remember I was on a call with a Helper in Florida, who was having a difficult time mitigating a talk between two neighbors who'd been quarreling since they arrived weeks prior. In the end, I was able to discern that the neighbors were actually in love with each other; but they both had been alone so long, they didn't know how to communicate their feelings for one another or notice the other person felt the same. It was really quite sweet!

When the call was over, I was called into my sister's office and told that I would no longer be working in the call center. Of course, I was absolutely outraged. Whenever I tended to do well in a position, I was transferred. I could never make the connection to every situation coming back to my sister, but I always had the hunch. Clara refused to have somebody else's light dim her own, or maybe it was because she didn't ever trust me–either way, it was the crux of our strained relationship for years. The innocent sibling rivalry turned sour long ago, and I couldn't figure out how to get us to a better place. More often than not, I kept away from her. When I received this assignment, my first time out in the field, I leapt for joy because the notice came from my sister's superior rather than her. I really thought I'd gotten out from under her thumb, as she never approved of my desire for baking or wishing to change divisions. She was the only one to know those wishes, and she tormented me for them ever since.

I sighed and rubbed my temples, the curled ringlets covering my entire face as I willed myself to take deep breaths, and try not to expect the worst so quickly. My sister wouldn't have the nerve to take me off my first real case before I barely get a footing, would she?

Lifting my head again, I adjust the red monstrosity that is my hair back from my face and sit up straighter. As always, I would do my best to be the bigger Elf here–my sister wouldn't take this away from me–no matter how much authority she has. She'd respect me by the time this was all done, when I'd figured out the cause and reversal of the Christmas Spirit depletion here in Everly Cove, and she'd eat her words from last Christmas Eve about how I wasn't going anywhere with my life. She'd see, they all would.

"If Clara thought it wise for me to have further Elf assistance, I would believe it to be for a good enough cause. What is it she asked you here for?"

Izabelle took a few sips of her soup, a combination of mushroom and potato I hadn't had a chance to dive into yet, and straightened in her seat, pulling a knee up to rest her arm upon as she spoke.

"Clara thought you'd need backup...somebody who could help manage things and make the quick decision to pull out if necessary. Apparently, the town has grown incredibly suspicious of the various café owners throughout the years; nobody has been able to blend in with the people enough to not raise questions and apprehension. The opening is a big deal, this is really our last opportunity to discover the cause of the energy crisis here." Izabelle paused and tapped the table awkwardly, altering her voice to sound more sincere with her next words. "Hey, I don't think she meant anything by it, I think she wants to help. I'll be able to run the café, keep appearances, and warm up to the locals without raising eyebrows. I may look rough around the edges, but I know how to sweet talk; it's one of my specialties. My magic makes it so people naturally feel more comfortable and persuadable around me, it's why your sister asked me instead of someone else."

Izabelle's explanation did make sense, but it still rubbed me the wrong way to know, even with this, that my sister was making decisions for me, deeming me unworthy to navigate this situation on my own. But I needed help; it was clear I wouldn't be able to run the café efficiently and snoop around enough to make a dent in the ever-growing mystery here. I needed Izabelle, and Clara knew that.

I forced my best fake smile and stood, having lost my appetite as the conversation went on. I grabbed my coat and went to hang it and my ear muffs on the coat rack by the front door. Turning to Izabelle, I pushed up the sage green sleeves of my sweater past my elbows, and clapped my hands, simultaneously waking Gimli with an annoyed growl.

"Alright then! Let's get this café open!"

3

Expectations A Plenty

Colby

I finished my errands and was already making my way back to town hall. After the odd interaction at the post office, I had a difficult time getting the quirky red-headed girl off my mind. I'd never seen her before, and when she told me she was the new café owner, I thought it made absolutely perfect sense.

All the past owners over the years never lasted, and I think it was because they didn't seem like people who would run a coffee shop at all. One guy was so stuck up, and even quite the germaphobe, I once watched him cry when a little girl accidentally skipped into him, leaving a mess of some berry pie all over his khaki pants. He was gone within the week. The others weren't that extreme, but they were so serious and didn't seem to find a single ounce of joy at the work. I would often have to go pick up large coffee orders for the office, and it was always the same. The owners weren't very personable, they looked agitated about something that had nothing to do with espresso or cookies.

But this one, Ms. Tinsel, she was bubbliness personified, not to mention sass. It left a placeholder in my mind ever since she sarcastically noted she wished to no longer be in my presence.

What a bewitchingly vexing girl.

She'd cause a man a headache in an hour–her sharp mouth wrapped in an adorably curvaceous body. I may be sworn off to lovers or girlfriends of any type, but it doesn't mean I don't notice a stunning girl who suddenly appears in this town.Which in all honesty, was incredibly refreshing. She was nothing like any girls around here–all prim and proper in one regard, and in another, absolute bitterness and lack of feelings–the little sirens. All looks on the outside, shallow pools of intellect and emotions on the inside. Which is exactly why I haven't had a real relationship in 2 years.

People here avoided me and my bad attitude at all costs; they never speak up when I am overly rude, or downright complacent. I am usually left alone, and it was better for me this way. Being the mayor's son was not as easy as people assumed. Especially if you are the ungrateful son who wished to leave Everly Cove rather than succeed it as its next mayor; which was my father's only goal in life.

For me, Everly Cove has grown to be more of a thorn than a rose in recent years. A thorn I so eagerly wished to rid myself of, rather than see for another minute longer. The cold irritated my skin, I wished for sunshine when it remained cloudy and grey as often as possible, and it took everything in me to not break down every single time the holidays came back around.

My father is, and always has been, oblivious to my unwillingness to go into the family legacy. As long as there have been

Jacksons in Everly Cove—which is almost as long as America was established—Jackson men have continuously held a political position in the community. Particularly a mayoral one. My father's dream was to pass this on to his only child, and I was the disappointment that kept trying to run away every chance I got.

That is, until 5 years ago. When the air I breathed was knocked out of me for good, solidifying my father and I's already tainted relationship even more. We drove each other apart further than we already were, and yet I haven't been able to bring myself to run away again. Not this time. The ghosts here haunt me daily, but it was also that very reason it was too hard to say goodbye for good.

I've stayed as my father's assistant, holding back the hatred of his job for a paycheck, putting away every cent I could in hopes that I'll have the courage to leave this place once and for all. But the years keep passing, and I'm still here, filing paperwork, mailing letters, and maintaining a life of solitude without any progression. I'm stuck, and I've known this. I'm 32 and unable to mingle with a large group of friends, unable to make serious and real connections with a woman in years, and unable to let the haunting spirits leave me be enough to get my ass out of here and start fresh.

And how many times do you have to "start fresh" to realize perhaps you don't have anything you're particularly good at enough to do or go anywhere other than here?

That damned insufferable, degrading voice that tormented me on the daily was becoming more unbearable with each passing day. The self-shame mounted higher than the surging waves that ravished the shoreline whenever storms passed, and I swear if it wasn't for this nagging companion, I'd have the strength to leave already. But the good memories linger too, amidst the heartache. They don't talk about that part of the grieving process enough. The combined need to move on and let go, but the continuous pounding in your chest every time you remember something good, how the aching dulls and you long to be with the familiar. Even if they can't be with you.

I'm interrupted in my brooding thoughts when Zeus barks at my feet. I didn't notice we'd already arrived back at town hall, and I'd neglected to open the door. Zeus was impatient when it came to his adoring public, especially the doting clerk who greeted people at the front desk. She was his favorite here and he never missed an opportunity to beg for treats. When I still wasn't quick enough, he barked again.

"Hey, hey calm down. Alright. You know, you could at least pretend to have a little self-respect. It's a bit pathetic to show you want something so bad."

Zeus was a gentle giant with everyone else, but when it came to me, he'd jump on me to get his way in a heartbeat. I wasn't about to ruin these jeans though, so I opened the town hall door and he sauntered inside, carefree and welcomed with bright smiles and gentle loving.

Must be life, hm? Greeted like you're somebody's favorite person to see.

I left Zeus to get his much-undeserved attention; but who could blame him; everybody in town adored Zeus. He was the town mascot at this point. I nodded quietly to Jeanine, the clerk who'd been around since the start of my father's campaign almost 20 years ago.

Out of the corner of my eye, I watched Zeus do a handshake for a goldfish cracker and shook my head, but a smile eased my stern features as I made my way down the hall to my father's personal office.

Approaching a large wooden door that appeared cracked open, I try to release the tension in my shoulders and prepare for the always lovely and completely demeaning interaction with my father that I attempt to avoid whenever possible. But, I'd been asked to meet him here by his secretary while I was out, and I dreaded discovering what the meeting was about this time. A gruff clearing of a throat let me know I was allowed to enter the office.

My father, what a way with words.

When I opened the door, my father sat hunched behind his desk flipping through a mound of paperwork. For a man in his late 50s, he was in incredible shape. Dressed in a fine black suit and emerald tie, his perfectly coiffed hair is neatly in place, his salt and pepper beard making him look even more distinguished. It was definitely not a surprise that a lot of the single women around here did their absolute most to gain his attention. They always wondered if he'd find another wife. But in the end, they were all greeted with the same lifeless, politician smile and discouraged pat on the shoulder. The day he remarries, will be the day snow stops falling permanently in Maine. I'll need to see it to believe it.

This, in retrospect, was one of the only things I did respect about him. The fact he hasn't immediately moved on from my mother. I know he's a grown man, fully capable of making his own decisions in life, but it would feel as though the dagger was being driven deeper than it already was. I could hardly live here as is, let alone if I saw him canoodling with another woman right in front of me. His love for her above all else, ran deeper than most anything. We did connect on that regard, at the very least. Which really might be the only reason we tolerated each other in the first place. Our mutual love for my mother was the only thing we had in common. I only wished it brought us closer rather than wedged the gap between us more. But, life isn't always like the movies: there isn't always a happy ending after tragedy, where the family reunites in their mutual loss.

My father continued to scribble signatures on sealed documents, entirely ignoring my presence at the meeting *he* asked for.

Same old Dad, making everyone wait upon him.

After several more minutes, my frustration grew beyond my capacity to be cordial. With more indignation than I should've allowed to slip through, I coughed and unapologetically let out an exasperated sigh.

"Dad, what did you want? You so graciously tasked me with a million errands today, could we please hurry this along? It's nearly the end of the day and I'd like to begin my off time that every employee so rightly deserves."

Theodore Jackson stood up and raised an eyebrow at me, as though I interrupted a much too important thought. Straightening his tie leisurely, he spoke as though it was I, who called for this.

"Colby, my boy, the mayoral family doesn't take time off. You know this. Which is what brings me to why I called you here. I need you to attend an event in an hour—the new re-opening of the coffee shop. I was just reading the business license and I think that this time the coffee shop will be quite a rising success! The new owner appears to be incredibly dedicated and impeccably witty. She had the idea to allow pets. How genius! So many of our great townsfolk have pets they love to take with them everywhere; I'm excited to see what revenue this new venture holds! I, however, have an important dinner with the town council about future development plans, and I need you to go to the event in my stead–with Zeus of course."

I wasn't usually one to yell, or even raise my voice, but this man was bringing me to my absolute wits end. Each day brought a new clarity to life: there would be no other course. I'd have to follow in my father's footsteps no matter what. I had nothing else, no one else, and he knew that. He would take advantage and make sure there would be no opportunities other than the ones he presented. He didn't care about how I never wished to be mayor, or even live in this town past the age of 20. He didn't understand that the only reason I stayed these last years was because I was too afraid to lose every semblance of a decent memory of the one woman in my life who loved me unconditionally. He'd use my hurt for his gain, just as he always had. I'd be forced into this profession one way or another–he'd make sure of it.

No matter how many arguments we've had since my mother's death, he couldn't hear me–the cries for help and the desperate need for affection from him so that I may be able to move on. No. All he cared for was Everly Cove now; he made that clear years ago.

To fight him was pointless. I was his show boy, the handsome sidekick on the road to taking over his duties permanently. It's the very reason why he's gradually stepped away from smaller events and sent me instead. An entire calculated plan for controlling my life. I rubbed the back of my neck with a sighed, staring at the floor, gathering my strength to look up at him and meet his eyes with as much contempt as I could.

"Of course. A Jackson is always here to serve his constituents. Even when he knows it's nothing but deceit."

With that, I turned on my heels, leaving my father's angered eyes behind me, and went to find Zeus in the lobby.

4

Cinnamon Rolls & Slip of Tongues

Ginger

I zabelle and I worked hard for the last several hours, hurriedly trying to get everything together for the grand opening of the shop. I was dotting every carrot nose on the snowman sugar cookies I baked, she was adding fairy twinkle lights strung up all over the café, and Gimli was hanging around a batch of batter still set on the counter, trying to decide if he'd be able to take a paw to the remainder leftovers before I catch him. But I knew the fiend all too well, and scolded over my shoulder at him as I finished the final touches of the cookie and set it on the display rack with the others.

"Gimli...you know that isn't for you. I have plenty of cat treats cooling, wait 2 minutes and you can have a few, okay?"

Gimli meowed and I laughed in response; always the impatient cat. He'd said that he enjoys the batter, which I don't blame him, but that he'd wait even if it might starve him. He swished his white tipped black tail in a manner that suggested he was accentuating for effect, and jumped off the counter heading to see what Izabelle was up to. Calling after him mockingly, I bring the tray of cookies to place inside the glass case under the coffee station, setting it neatly next to the miniature quiches, blueberry pie slices, and the croissants that'd just come out of the oven, the decadent scent still hanging in the air.

"Ever the dramatic feline, hm?"

Looking around the café, my delicious concoctions are beautifully prepared and organized. There were bags of cat and dog treats with little red and green ribbons to cinch the tops, sitting inside a basket at the front of the shop, and the string lights and instrumental jazz Christmas music to set the ambiance. The excitement of what we were doing was beginning to surge through me. Even though my sister sent Izabelle to help, I was still in charge of how this operation would run. For the very first time in my life, this was totally mine. My stamp, sealing the start of an epic adventure sure to allow me the life I always dreamt of. And I was able to bake! My greatest desire was here, actualized in a legitimate storefront. I am getting the opportunity to incorporate something I love, and watch others enjoy it.

This was surreal. My first mission was about to officially begin! My heart thudded inside my chest as I checked the time on the old clock above the door. Izabelle told me a few minutes ago that it looked like a crowd was forming in the center of the square, all waiting for us to open our doors.

My heart pounded at the news, but there wasn't time to panic—it was now or never; this was the first real impression the town would get of me. I needed to make it count, otherwise I'd never be able to gather the intel I needed to save this town and the North Pole.

I quickly grabbed a handful of treats and placed them on the table perch I made for Gimli for the event. He thanked me and began eating them, unaware or unwilling to care that a swarm of people would be entering in mere minutes.

What if I can't do this?

Darn that pesky inner voice! This was the absolute worst time. Usually, I found myself to be incredibly confident, always being able to be adaptable to any given situation or role I needed to play back at Headquarters. But here, in the middle of pretending to be a human surrounded by lots of other humans, I would have to say that I am seriously scared out of my mind! Not to mention, this was secretly the first time I'd be displaying my baking skills in such a way.

Back home, I only ever baked for my family; my little sisters forever raved that if I could open my own bakery in the Pole, I would have the best one around! My father is always quick to eat and not so quick to compliment despite how many cookies or macaroons he'd stow away in his pockets for later. My mom was the one who continuously kept showing me new recipes; she also loved to bake. I always thought that perhaps it was a dream of hers as well to become a baker, but she never voiced it. She only brought out another old recipe book, or quietly asked to help decorate the assortment of cupcakes I made earlier. I found her to be watching whenever I baked, a longing look flickering behind her eyes. Perhaps she was just as stuck as I was. The thought made my heart hurt for her, because we couldn't leave our station no matter how talented we were. It was the worst and saddest part of being an Elf. Now my sister, on the other hand, hardly ever ate what I baked. In a way, I wondered if she was too jealous that I had the gift to mold dough into playful sensations, or create the cutest of reindeer on sugar cookies that would make you slap Santa!

Either way, it was only ever my family who tried my creations. The anticipation of whether others would enjoy them, was almost making me sick to my stomach.

Izabelle must've seen me waver on my feet and rushed towards me, dropping the end of the string lights she'd been wrapping around the entryway. She skidded to a halt and looked at me all over, her hands on my shoulders.

"Ginger, are you good? You look like you're going to fall over."

I shook my head yes. "Yeah, I'm okay. Sorry, I wasn't expecting to get so nervous before the opening."

Izabelle glanced around and sighed. "It's going to be great. You have everything set up and you're not alone. Your sister told me you're one of the best workers, you're super quick on your feet and your energy lights up a room; everybody is going to love you, your goodies, and you're going to crack this case." Pausing momentarily, the tinge of excitement in her voice had me surprised, but she quickly glanced down and shrugged her shoulders coolly. "You gotta relax, or they will be able to tell something's off, okay? They have become too suspicious of the other agents over the years, we have to be ready."

I moved my hair out of my eyes and looked at Izabelle, who was a good few inches taller than me; she was far more passable for a human than I was. Her dark eyes met mine and I was so confused by her words.

She's right...playtime is over. It's Ginger time now, and I have to be at my best to make this happen.

I nearly jumped out of my skin when a knock came from the door. My eyes darted to that old clock on the wall and we were already a couple minutes late to opening the doors.

Great start, Ginger.

I looked at Izabelle, unable to formulate a response to her kind words and then her equally terrifying reality check right after. I shook my head to shake away the doubt, pulled my shoulders back and marched towards the door to let the guests inside and start this long-anticipated opening, and the true beginning of my mission.

I opened the door to a line that went out towards the street, and I couldn't stop myself from smiling. A woman with a bright red nose from the cold, who wore a navy coat and matching hat, smiled broadly at me. The lady couldn't be much older than me, but the way she dressed would make one assume otherwise. She had a camera that hung around her neck by a strap and her glasses lay lopsided on her nose.

"Hi! Oh goodness, we were starting to wonder if we got the date wrong for the opening! I'm Miriam Conters, a photographer for the local newspaper, the Everly Herald, I'm so excited to be covering this assignment! Are you ready for us?"

As ready as I'll ever be!

"Absolutely! Let's get you all out of the cold!"

Miriam walked inside, and when I looked over my shoulder, I saw Gimli had surprisingly gotten off his perch and was making his way towards the door to greet the customers. I smiled at him and he gave a meow of consent, letting me know I owed him one for his hospitality. Chuckling to myself, I waved the line of about 20 or more people in through the door, shaking gloved hands, passing hellos and "Sorry to keep you waiting!" or a "Thank you so much for coming out today!" as one by one, they entered **Tinsel Brews & Sweets,** and that momentary panic began to fade away. Several swooshy tails of little doggos sauntered by me, and each one greeted me pleasantly, not that their owners would know; and even one cat carried in a luxurious carrier, was set down and introduced itself to Gimli—who to my shock, meowed a lovely hello and began walking to show the other cat around the shop.

As they walked by, I counted 20 people in total, 4 dogs, and 1 cat. I was absolutely blown away by the turn out! Although we definitely were all a little snug, it felt lively and cozy. Chattering had already started among the guests, who all seemed to find the new name to be adorable, and I heard murmurs of how delicious the baked goods I'd prepared looked behind the glass case. One man mumbled that he wondered how long it would be until he could get his coffee.

Once everyone was comfortable either taking seats at tables or booths, or standing along the wall, Izabelle was already set up behind the coffee station, ready to go when orders came in. I weaved my way through to stand in front of the coffee station where I had hung a large red bow that strung across from the wall, and waited until the whispers settled as I stood before the crowd.

"Good afternoon, everyone! I am so happy to have you here for the opening! My name is Ginger Tinsel, and I'd like to welcome you to the newly renamed, Tinsel Brews & Sweets!" A light applause came, seeming to mostly be initiated by Izabelle.

Well, she did say her magic enabled her to get people to become more comfortable.

I cleared my throat and continued on with my much practiced speech that I'd written before I arrived in town and practiced vigorously in the bathroom mirror the night before.

"It's an honor to move to this beautiful town and become a part of your great community today! I'm also from a small town in Minnesota, and after going to culinary school there, I decided to make the leap to start my own business in another small town with strong roots. I hope that my unique take on a coffee house experience by allowing pets, will be one that you find enjoyable. I also hope that you will enjoy the many treats you'll get to experience here that are all homemade and fresh daily!"

I stared at a lot of blank faces, all of whom were skeptical of my speech. It made sense, they'd had several new developers here in the last years, and none of them made the cut with the townspeople. I cleared my throat again and turned to reference Izabelle.

"I'd love to introduce my business partner and the day-to-day manager here at Tinsel's, Izabelle Pepperidge. You want delicious coffees, she's your go to!" I luckily got a couple of laughs from that one. Leaning over the counter, I grab a pair of scissors and make a final announcement.

"Tinsel's is now open! Everybody please come and place your orders!"

I proceeded to cut the ribbon, letting it fall to the floor with an unexpected applause and several howls from the dogs. I laughed to myself and stepped out of the way, a line already forming in front of Izabelle as the espresso machine fires up and she starts the orders. Walking around, I meet several of the people; first it's Joanne and Martin Lindley, they run the hardware store nearby and brought their German Shepherd, Max, with them. They chatted with me asking about my interest in Everly Cove and somehow bought my story from before. I patted Max's head and offered him a bag of free treats to take home with them. They both shook my hand and patted me on the back, before taking their lattes to a table in the back to sit awhile.

After speaking to several others, including the kind owners of both the nearby bookstore and the small grocery market, I handed out a tray of free samples of my famous cinnamon rolls. As I was making my rounds, I was tapped on the shoulder by kind brown eyes, a woman with dark brown hair in an updo, a tie-dyed headband sat prominently on her head, the silky ends of it falling down the back of her neck. Her ears were decorated with the most beautiful turquoise earrings that dangled. The woman wore a grey sweater underneath an emerald green kimono that draped past her knees; she immediately felt like a kindred spirit, and my shoulders eased at her company.

"Excuse me, Ginger? I'm Annie, I run the post office across the street. My nephew told me earlier that you came by to drop a letter off and I was unavailable. I just wanted to apologize! I ran to the store to grab a quick lunch and I always forget that sign to let people know I'll be back later!"

The reminder of the blatantly rude gentleman back at the post office earlier that morning already felt like a lifetime ago, but the sting of his attitude still made me huff in irritation.

"Yes! I did come by, it's not a problem! I can tend to be forgetful myself, and your nephew was most *gracious*."

I covered my mouth, surprised that I'd let out so much snark to a stranger like that. Something about that man really riled me up!

"Oh gosh, I didn't mean it that way.."

Annie let out a bold laugh and held her stomach, laughing so hard, she could barely catch a breath.

"Gracious my dear, there isn't a thing you need to apologize for! My nephew can be a prickly beast on a good day. He's like one of those sour candies, where it's sweet long after the initial burst of bitterness wears off. He's a tough one to crack, and I'm not surprised his welcoming was something left to be desired. He's a good boy, he just tends to leave his manners at home."

For the first time since arriving in Everly Cove, I felt myself relax. Annie wasn't upset at my slipping up with dissing her nephew, she assured me my reaction must've been common. Her lively attitude was a breath of fresh air. With the stakes so high for this mission, maybe it wouldn't be so hard to find friends here, and not just a way to save the Christmas Spirit.

"Thank goodness! I was afraid of being rude about your own nephew."

Annie nodded and took a sip of her coffee she was holding. "Ah my dear, no one can be ruder than that sourpuss. But, the boy is handsome though. It's a true shame he hasn't found a pretty girl like you yet!"

The tray of samples I'd been holding fumbled in my fingertips at Annie's comment. The silver platter was already tumbling out of my hands and towards the ground before I could use my magic to stop it; small objects could be easily caught if done so quickly without raising much suspicion–play it off as having incredible luck–instead the entire tray splattered on the ground. The slices of cinnamon roll I baked earlier flooded at Annie and I's feet.

Shaking my head I rushed down to the ground. "Gosh, excuse me. I'm so sorry, butter fingers I gues–" Hurriedly picking up the pieces of cinnamon roll, my brain was scrambling at Annie's mention of me being a beautiful girl, and on top of that, that her absolutely unpleasant nephew—who although was probably one of the most good-looking guys I've ever seen—made my pulse skitter at the mention of him being with a girl like me. Another hand came into eyesight, helping pick up several of the pieces. When I was about to look up and thank whoever it was, Annie's voice came ringing in the background of my frantic thoughts.

"Oh, speak of the Devil."

The pit of my stomach tumbled at her words. When I looked up, her nephew was kneeling right before me, cinnamon roll fragments in hand, staring directly into my eyes with those perfect honeyed ones of his. My heart stopped entirely.

5

Photoshoots &
Contempt

Colby

When I started picking up destroyed pastry near my Aunt, who I was meeting at the new Tinsel café, I didn't realize that the one girl I was most hoping to run into again–and also chiding myself to avoid–would be the one who created the mess in the first place.

She runs the café, dummy. How would you avoid her here?

When I met her emerald eyes as she hastily blurted out apologies, her movements stopped when she realized who was helping her, as did mine. For a split second, the noise of the café, the music, the chatter of townspeople, the dogs panting and cat meows, and hissing of the espresso machine–all of it fell away. I felt completely frozen, stuck in place by that piercing gaze.

Ms. Tinsel had the cutest little button nose, and freckles that playfully danced upon her cheeks. Her lips were luscious, and I could smell the peppermint lip balm she wore that sparkled in the light. When the last of the spell wore off, my eyes were unable to move from her mouth where she bit her bottom lip, totally unaware of how I was watching them so intently. It wasn't done in a seductive way, more an involuntary nervous habit; and God did it somehow make it even more attractive that she was so unaware of her beauty–*or how it was affecting me.*

I placed the remainder of the pieces I'd picked up on her tray, and we both stood simultaneously. It wasn't hard to see that the pulse in her neck had quickened, and if I hadn't known any better, I would've said she was equally as thrown by the interaction as I was. My aunt however, was completely oblivious as she pulled me around to place a large kiss on my cheek, and it felt like one of those embarrassing moments from middle school where you got affection from a parent in front of the popular kids. I wasn't usually one to wish to hide away from a beautiful woman, but in this moment, I wondered if there was a way I could shrink myself and dart off as fast as possible.

"Colby! Ah, I was wondering when you were going to show up! Your ears must've been burning because Ginger and I were just talking about you."

Ginger.

I finally heard her first name, and the way it hung in the air made it feel like I could pluck it off a tree like an apple, and when I'd go to take a bite, I knew it would be the sweetest thing to ever grace my lips. The name, like the profession, fit her perfectly. Like when you meet someone and hear their name and go "Wow! You look like a so-and-so!"

Ginger only continued to look at me, so I decided to break the tension and do my best to slip back into the persona I'd carried so well over the last few years—aloof and distanced.

"Oh goody, I'm sure it was a riveting conversation." My eyes finally pulled away from Ginger, and the nonchalant, cool Colby was back. And this Colby had zero time or energy for small talk.

"Actually, we were only getting started! Pity I couldn't tell Ginger more about your incredible charms. I know you hide them so well. Another time then. I almost forgot!" Annie turned back to Ginger and patted her arm, as if she was an old friend already. A pang of jealousy I was unaware of blindsided me; I may be cold, but my aunt was the closest thing to my mother I had left. One of the only reasons I'd survived the grief over the years at all, was by maintaining a strong relationship with her. Somehow this girl who showed up out of nowhere, was already winning her over. Not that that was a difficult thing to do; everybody loved Annie, and now it seemed everyone was going to adore Ginger just as much.

"Ginger, darling, a few of the other business owners in town wanted me to invite you to the annual Christmas Business Banquet. We do it every year to celebrate our fellow entrepreneurs, and this year it's at the Harbor Restaurant & Inn on the coast where the lighthouse is! We are having dinner there. Ha, it's going to be a blast! We know you're new to the community, but from the looks of it, I believe after all these years, we are going to have a hip joint for coffee and treats! I'd love it if you'd be able to come, it's this Saturday. Also, do you think you'd be able to bake us a cake for the event? I know it's last minute, but your chocolate eclairs are absolutely divine! I'd love to see what you could do with a cake!"

Ginger blushed a bright red which nearly matched her flaming curls that now, without the absurd fuzzy earmuffs, frayed around her cheeks. One curl fell in her face and she quickly brushed it aside. I clenched my jaw to keep from staring again.

"Of course, Annie. I'd love to come, and I'd be more than happy to make a cake for the event."

Annie hugged Ginger tightly and clapped her hands in excitement.

"Great! I'll let the others know! Alright now, you two youngins, I'll be off. Fantastic opening, Ginger! It's so nice to finally have some Christmas joy in town again, almost reminds me of the festival days we had that everyone misses so much. And Colby...behave yourself."

Annie was off, and I was left standing beside Ginger awkwardly.

Ginger at last looked at me and smiled. "Your aunt is incredibly kind. I already feel so welcomed here. Also, thank you for helping clean up my mess. In all honesty, I'm surprised you're here. After your incredibly rude comment about my establishment, after all."

There it was, the sharp wit that made her so captivating to me at the post office. Usually, I would've responded in a playful manner, but my insides were already boiling at the instant affection my aunt gave Ginger. Despite my best efforts, I found myself outrageously angry.

"I wouldn't be here unless I had to be, *Cupcake*. Trust me."

Ginger's eyes filled with irritation, her brows furrowing, her mouth slightly open in dismay; but I wasn't sure if it was my callus tone or the nickname.

"**Don't** call me that. And don't let the door hit you on the way out. I may enjoy the company of your lovely aunt, but doesn't mean I need to have a desire to do anything with you, *Colby*. So if you'll excuse me, I have customers to assist. Good day."

A part of my heart ached at how quickly she wished me away, not that this reaction wasn't normal; I tended to push everyone away in the end. Perhaps I was just getting her out of the way sooner than usual, even if it did make that endless regret resurface the instant she looked at me like I was a disgusting monster rather than anyone she might've liked. It didn't matter, it was better this way.

Ginger swiveled on her heels and almost ran directly into Miriam Conters, the town photographer.

"There you are! This is going so great, Ginger! Mind if we get some photos of you now? I've already gotten some candid shots of the customers and Izabelle of course, who by the way is a dollface!"

I rolled my eyes and began making my way out of the café. I'd left Zeus at home despite my father's request to take him, as I was hoping this wouldn't take much of my time; luckily I was right. Ginger flared a stare in my direction, and cast her eyes downward before responding to Miriam.

"Sure, Miriam. Where do you want me?"

Miriam scrambled to push Ginger away from me towards the coffee station, and I couldn't help but linger a moment longer to watch as Miriam positioned her where she wanted, when I suddenly heard my name being called.

"Colby! Yes, this will be perfect! I'd love to get you in a few shots with Ginger, you know, shaking hands, welcoming her to the town, that sort of thing."

And before I could promptly tell her no, she was whizzing by me, circling around and pushing my back from behind to stand closely to Ginger–***too close.***

When I felt Ginger's head against my chest from the sheer force of how hard Miriam pushed us together to get her shots, I felt like it might combust right then and there. Ginger cleared her throat and looked around, clearly uncomfortable with the contact as well.

"Um...excuse me Miriam, but is Colby here as like, showing me with a customer–because I'm pretty sure I could pose with someone else."

Miriam chuckled and pulled her camera hanging from her neck in front of her eyes.

"No! It's going to be so great to get you with the mayor's son in a photo! I bet it'll even make the front page; and I've never made it to the front page before! Okay you two, big smiles for me on 3...2..1.."

When Miriam was about to snap the photo, Ginger pulled away, a confused look on her face.

"Mayor's son?!"

Then her eyes met mine, and the whirring of Miriam's camera blinded everything else.

SNAP! FLASH! CLICK!

6

Hot & Cold

Ginger

It felt like a century before Miriam finished relentlessly posing Colby and I for photos. The one we were doing now, Miriam made us shake hands. A seemingly innocent action, but to me, it felt like fire to touch his hand. Every second we held each other's hands, I could feel my face getting hotter and hotter. Although I'm 29, I haven't had very good attempts at decent relationships. The last intimate interaction I had was over a year ago with another Elf named Simon, and it was short-lived, and the intimacy was not what I'd dreamt of. After that relationship I decided to focus solely on my career, because it never felt like I could find a worthwhile connection.

Although this man was one of the most irritating beings I've ever been around, he was also *hot.* So unfortunately for me, I had a major physical reaction towards him. Perhaps it was the long time between relationships or something else, but there was no denying it; I was insanely attracted to Colby, and yet, I could hardly speak a few words to him without the interaction going awry.

He's the mayor's son, too!

Oh yeah, I nearly fell on the floor in shock when Miriam announced that. How did I go through an entire conversation with his Aunt, and her not mention anything like that? I don't know what it was about Colby being the mayor's son that made me even more nervous to be around him, maybe I was more surprised at his uncaring attitude for *being* the son of the mayor. But from the looks of it, he despised doing anything related to helping out his dad, or being in the public eye.

From Annie's other comment about how the town has lacked Christmas joy for quite some time after the mayor declared no further decorating or Christmas festivals would happen. She was so happy to see I had decorated. So what was going on in this town as to why the mayor forced the Christmas festivals that brought in thousands a year and made Christmas Spirit sky-rocket, to now being nothing? And would Colby have something to do with this also?

There were a lot of questions, but I couldn't help but believe that the mayoral family might be at the center of all this dilemma. I needed to get to the bottom of it, which meant I needed to get closer to Colby to find out why. That thought alone, made my heart jump. Colby made me ridiculously nervous and frustrated at the same time. But he could be the key to solving this mystery.

Despite the awkward photoshoot with him, I did get invited to a dinner for the entrepreneurs in town, which could be my key to implementing Stage 2 of my plan. Now that I knew from Annie that the townspeople missed the festival, I would go to the meeting and submit for a renewal of it, wrapping the festival with a Christmas Yueltide Ball.

I'd go to the dinner, schmooze the locals, and try to get more information on why the festival stopped in the first place. Then I'd introduce my plans for bringing the festival back, and hopefully get one step closer to restoring the Christmas Spirit here. Annie's remarks gave me hope that the people would love to have the festivities back, and I think it'll be our best bet to increase energy levels here for the Pole.

I was brought out of my scheming when Colby stepped on my foot.

"Ouch! Could you mind your ginormous feet, please?"

I wondered in the back of my mind if I'd been a bit harsh, but something about Colby forced the sarcastic, rude version of me forward, rather than my usual bubbly and agreeable personality. It was only one of the long list of reasons why I wasn't sure if getting closer to him would be a good idea; I don't know how much I like myself around him.

Colby threw his hands up in sarcastic defense.

"Sorry, Cupcake, you're just so small I keep forgetting you're even there."

I huffed loudly and looked up at him, his amber eyes making me trip over my words.

"Ugh! Would you stop calling me Cupcake?"

Colby rolled his eyes, his square-framed glasses falling slightly on his nose. He pushed them back up and looked at Miriam.

"Hey Mir, are we done? I need to get going."

I was relieved to not be the one to say it, but I'm fairly certain Miriam got about 1000 photos of us; more than enough in my opinion.

"Oh yeah, sorry! I got a bit carried away; you two are absolutely stunning together! A fine couple you'd make. Yeah, you can head out, Colby. Thanks!"

Miriam snapped a final shot and walked away. When I looked around, the café had emptied almost completely already. There were only a few stragglers left sitting at tables, Izabelle looked to be putting stuff away in the back kitchen, and surprisingly I caught Colby staring at the Christmas decorations, unsure whether he liked or hated them.

Geez, we took pictures together for so long.

I found Gimli snoozing in a booth seat and there was no one else but us now. I didn't quite know what to say.

"Uhh...okay well, it's time for me to close up."

Colby seemed to have a mixture of disappointment and agitation at the sudden realization that we were alone together. I took a step back, not seeing I was still only a few inches away from him. My hands moved that annoying stray curl from my face again and I tugged the sleeves of my sweater. Colby still didn't move.

"Right. Congrats on your opening. I'll let my father know what a success it was. He was excited when your business plans came up. Goodnight.."

I shifted on my feet, doing what I could to look anywhere but those mesmerizing eyes of his.

"Thanks. You could've said something rude about it, and you didn't. So I appreciate that. I hope we can get along, for your Aunt's sake."

A temporary flash of calm sat in the air between us, but then his mood shifted again. Like the mention of his Aunt set him off.

"Don't act like you know what is good for my Aunt's sake or not. You may be the new golden girl around here, but you don't know anything about us to make statements like that. You should keep your nose out of it, Ginger."

Colby walked out of the café, hands in his pockets, leaving me standing there in the wake of his ice cold words. My annoyance with him flared again, the kind comment from before totally erased from my mind.

And I couldn't help but feel I wasn't sure my plan to get close enough to him to better understand why his dad stopped the Christmas festival years ago, would ever be possible. Because I couldn't stand him—not for a single second.

This was going to be harder than I thought.

7

Friendly Interference

Colby

"**M**an, she's gorgeous! How could you say something like that to her!?"

My friend Tom Jeffords, was currently needling me about the interaction I told him about with Ginger back at the opening. He'd been there, but with the commotion of photographs, I never got a chance to speak to him. Now, all I could do was chug my beer and hope he gives it a rest. He wasn't wrong; Ginger Tinsel was remarkable in such a different way than I was used to. But, she was also starting to become a pain in my ass, even if she was a pretty one at that.

"It's been years since a girl like that has come around this boring town. Come to think of it, I don't think I've ever seen a girl like Ginger. She's peppy, gorgeous, funny and everybody seems to love her already. She brings a vibrancy I haven't seen here in years, especially a vibrancy in *you*, Colby. There's no point denying it."

Damnit Tom, always the over-observant dick.

I finished my 2nd beer and placed it on the bar, waving to the bartender for another round. Jeremiah's was the only bar in town–a little hole in the wall, but inviting and cheery, and one of the only places other than running errands for dad and being home, I ever ventured to; which means it had become a habit going out with Tom like this, especially when I was upset about something.

"Look, it doesn't matter. You know I'm not interested in being with anybody, and to top it off, she's full of attitude. I mean, did you hear what she said to me about 'Annie's sake'?"

Tom took another sip of his vodka soda and raised a suggestive eyebrow at me.

"What I heard was that a girl got you riled up, Colby. And I think, in more ways than one."

God if he wasn't always right somehow.

I couldn't even find the words to refute what Tom said. I knew deep down that I've been hooked by this girl, and she hadn't even shown to find my company pleasant in the slightest. Tom was also right when he said she was a vibrant light that hadn't glowed in Everly Cove in years. Not since my own mother shined upon the town–especially during Christmas.

Ginger's coffee shop, draped in twinkle lights and wreaths, filled with Christmas cookies and ribbons, made the town feel–for the first time in years–like it used to. When every shop was dolled up in ornaments and greenery, the town square radiated with lights of all colors all over the main courtyard, and the Christmas festival went on for weeks, different events littering the days with joy and good times. Ever since my father banned the Christmas festival after my mother's death, the town's overall demeanor plummeted, with not so much as a bow on a front door to commemorate the holidays. It was one of the saddest things I could think of, and seeing Ginger's sweet treats and jovial nature light up the spirits of every townsperson in there today, made my heart leap at the thought of all those happy times coming back again.

Except you're forgetting the one person who won't be there to enjoy it with you.

The memory of my mom forced bile to the back of my throat. I willed it down and thanked the bartender when he returned with another drink. I fiddle with the foam of my beer and find my thoughts wandering back to those hazel eyes and that wild red hair that I itched to run my hands through. Clearly Tom noticed and sighed heavily.

"You can't be alone forever. I know you miss your mom, but she wouldn't want you wasting your life chasing after her ghost. She would want you to move on, find a nice girl, and settle down or go explore the world again. She wouldn't want you to lose your life just because she lost hers."

I shook my head in frustration, "But what if I'm not meant for anything other than this?"

A sadness filtered behind Tom's voice–he was truly a good friend. "Is that what you think?"

I wasn't sure. I hoped that I wouldn't be this miserable for the rest of my life. But one year turned into two, and two turned into 5; and here I was still miserable and alone in Everly Cove. No relationship that lasted, no goal out of here or a career to shift to–and an endless disappointment to my dad, who never saw me for who I really was. To stay here was becoming self-inflicted torture. I wasn't contributing to anything, and I wasn't finding joy. My mother would weep for me if she wasn't in her beach oasis I know she's at right now. She'd scold me for putting my dreams on hold and not settling down in a loving relationship. So if that's what she would want for me, why wasn't I able to change it? I rubbed the back of my neck and leaned back in the bar stool.

"I don't want to think that. Truly. You know how I feel about Everly Cove...you know what my relationship is like with my father. There's a lot holding me here, and yet, I want more than this. A week ago I almost filled out that application for a culinary school in New York, but every time I sit to do it, I feel that guilt eating away at me. I still feel her here, Tom. I don't know what I need to do to let her go, but I can't yet."

Tom knew my dream was to be a chef–I'd always had a passion for it. I used to make the meals for every fraternity house event and I got placed in a local magazine article for it, saying: I was a budding culinary expert that any restaurant would die to have in their kitchen. But my dad always had other plans for me, which is why I never spoke on the topic often other than to Tom. He was the one who forced us to have weekly dinners just so I didn't lose the skills, and he could get a free meal out of it. Tom sips his drink and slaps the top of his thighs dramatically.

"Fine, fine...stay longer. We will figure out when the time feels right, okay? But who's to say you can't finally have a little fun while you're here, huh?? As your best friend, I'm forcing you to make a connection with Ginger. There's going to be no fighting me on this; you desperately need to let loose, and she is chock-full of stress relief if I've ever seen. I have a good feeling about her, and you can't say you aren't a little intrigued. So your homework assignment is to go back to her shop, and apologize to her. See where things go after! Got it?"

I raise my eyebrow at him and mock the near doctor-like prescription he just gave me.

"Oh right, and I'll just pop over there for a spot of tea and light breakfast then, hm?"

Tom stands up abruptly and slaps my back, forcing me out of my stool and guiding me to the door.

"Breakfast?? Nu uh, dude. You're going *now!*"

8

Late Night Baking

Ginger

G imli meowed angrily at me from across the café. It was nearing 9pm and we were still here so I could prepare tomorrow's baked goods. I also needed to start planning the cake I'd be contributing to the Business Christmas Banquet happening this Saturday.

Plus, I was fuming! After this afternoon's events, and the infuriating attitude of Colby–who happened to turn out to be the one person in the town I desperately needed to get to know–I was stress baking to say the least. And Gimli was ready to go back to the cottage hours ago.

"Gimli, I'm sorry! You know I need to prepare for tomorrow, and now I'm making this elaborate cake for an event, and I feel already at my wits' end! Baking relieves me, you know that...can we stay a little longer?"

Gimli jumped up onto the kitchen counter and rubbed his body against my arm, letting me know he understood my anxiety. I smiled, and with my clean hand, rubbed his chin vigorously, then grabbed a cat treat to throw his way. He nipped it out of the air and happily walked back out to what has become his favorite sleeping spot in the window of the café, where I'd put a cat bed just for him.

I worked the dough that would make the pie crust for my potato-leek miniature pot pies that would be featured as tomorrow's main savory dish. I wiped my hands on my green and red striped apron I'd brought with me–it was nice to have a touch of home. It had red frills at the bottom and the top, and green ribbons that tied over my shoulders. The apron was my personal favorite, and I'd had so many fond memories using it growing up; I hoped it would bring me good luck here.

However, I was beginning to believe I'd need more of a Christmas miracle than pure luck. The thoughts of the day and how much was at stake were overflowing in my mind. Not to mention the absolute nightmare that was the full-out photoshoot with none other than the most exasperating man I'd ever met.

To top it off, this particular man was the closest connection to figuring out the mystery of the Christmas Spirit depletion. But after the interaction with him following the photoshoot, there was no way I'd be able to stand being in the same room with him for more than 5 seconds. He was rude. Unsavory. Completely oblivious to anyone else's feelings, and–if that weren't enough–he was...

A meow from Gimli let me know somebody was here right before a ring came from the front door.

At this time of night? In this small town? That can't be right.

I swooshed a hand at the direction of the boiling vegetables that sat in a large pot on the stove, which would be the filling for my savory pie. A large wooden spoon flew off the wall that held dozens of ladles, and went to stir the pot for me, and with a snap of my fingers, the stove lowered its heat to a simmer. Wiping my hands along the front of my apron, I walked out to the door. Gimli had already fallen back asleep, very much uninterested by the unexpected visitor, which he wouldn't have done if he was overly suspicious of whoever it was standing out in the cold.

I opened the door, and as the tinkling bell goes off above my head, I find Colby standing before me.

The shock of seeing him out in the snow, in the middle of the night, and *alone*, made me utterly confused.

"Colby! What a surprise...What are you doing here? You know we're closed right?"

Colby's amber-colored eyes glowed in the lamplight that hung on the outside of the café. He wore the same clothes as before from the opening. But despite the darkness and the snow that was picking up in flurries around him, those intoxicating honey eyes were now fully exposed, Colby having ditched his glasses from earlier–and I was all the more drawn in by them as he stared at me.

"Uh yeah, I know. I don't mean to intrude on your evening. I just was thinking I needed to come by to see if you were still here."

Folding my arms over my chest, I let my eyes fall to the ground, the awkwardness sitting in the air between us after our last encounter.

"I'm here, is something wrong?"

Colby rubbed his hands together, his gloves from earlier missing, and small puffs of air from his breath circled around him.

"Well...yes...I think so. I think we got off on the wrong foot. I never meant to be so rude to you...on both occasions we met. I'm not one to enjoy being in my father's limelight, and being put on the spot for photographs made me incredibly irritated. Which is by no means your fault, nor did you deserve for me to talk to you the way I did. I wanted to apologize to you, Ginger."

"Okay, so what is your excuse for the post office?"

Colby rubbed his neck and shook his head.

"I don't have one other than I was incredibly pigheaded, and I truly apologize."

I nodded in agreement.

"So pigheaded, I feared you may squeal at me like one."

He smirked at my insult like he found it amusing rather than hurtful.

"Ouch, I deserved that."

I wasn't exactly sure what to say to his apologies, but for sure couldn't leave him standing outside in the cold. Even if he did hurt my feelings a little bit before.

"Let's talk more inside. I can tell you're freezing."

I wave to him to come inside, and although he hesitates momentarily, he steps through the threshold wiping his boots on the doormat. Taking off his coat and scarf, he hangs them up beside the door.

"I'm sorry for barging in like this. I'm sure it's a surprise..."

You can say something like that...

"But I couldn't stop thinking about what I said to you at the opening. My mother would've beat me over the head with a spoon for the behavior, and I wouldn't have fared much better with my aunt. Anyways, I swear it wasn't intentional. I'm not often an enjoyable person to be around, but you just arrived here and I went all Scrooge on you in seconds."

His Scrooge joke made me laugh, and the corners of his eyes wrinkled in a smile at my reaction.

"I appreciate the apology, and yes, I'd say you were quite the Scrooge! Is it usual for you to greet all new people in town that way?"

He adjusted his glasses on the bridge of his nose, his movements a bit delayed, suggesting he'd had a drink before coming here. Although, it wasn't obnoxious to know, more adorable with his slightly flushed cheeks and eyes that shimmered with suggestion that made me desire to find out what was going on behind those mysterious eyes that called to me.

"Most days, but it's something I want to work on. Plus, we rarely get new people in town, let alone beautiful ones."

He covered his mouth, shocked at his own compliment. Coughing, he rubbed the back of his neck again, the green tone of his knit sweater that hung perfectly on his framed body, shifting in the light.

"Uhh...sorry. I'm not usually so cavalier."

I knew a blush was forming on my cheeks, and from the looks of it, Colby noticed too. I then remembered how absolutely ridiculous I must look right now, with this apron, the flour on my sweater, and the sensation that the top bun of my hair I'd hastily strung up, was half falling.

Beautiful? More like a chaotic mess!

"Don't worry about it..."

Another awkward silence fell between us. He did his best to look anywhere but me, but part of me couldn't help but smile. At last, he sniffed the air and made a "mmm" noise.

"Well, whatever you're making smells absolutely amazing right now. Is it typical for you to bake so late?"

"Sometimes! Depending on what I need to do...but I often stress bake. So I guess you can say that's what I'm doing."

Colby gave an apologetic look, grimacing slightly.

"That have something to do with me?"

If I was telling the truth, yes, to some capacity it was due to his insanely good looks and sour mood. But in reality, which he could never know, I was stressed about my mission. He could never know I was an actual Elf from the North Pole, and that the future of Christmas depended on me raising Christmas Spirit here in Everly Cove or there may not be Christmas in future years. Now for the first time though, hope rang through me like the ever so lovely jingle bells on Santa's sleigh; Colby was the son of the mayor, and from what Annie's suggestion inferred, the mayor stopped the Christmas festival. Colby would know why, and how to possibly get it back and running again. He was my best bet for figuring this out, so I needed to get to know him, and see what he might reveal about the town.

I casually shrug my shoulders.

"Maybe just a little bit...but you can make it up to me by giving me a hand?"

Colby rubbed his hands together and smiled broadly.

"Need a sous chef, eh?"

Chuckling, I waved him to follow me to the back kitchen, quickly remembering to stop the self-stirring spoon in the pot I'd left earlier. Usually after a certain point, I used my magic to pour the ingredients in, keep an eye on the time, or even shape dough. But tonight, we'd be doing it the old fashioned way–in hopes Colby might spend enough time to reveal a new piece of the puzzle of Everly Cove.

When we got back to the kitchen, I forgot just how tight and snug it was for two people to be back here together. Colby already rolled up his sleeves, and I found myself near him just as I was when taking the photographs, but this time, my shoulders were less tense, and the scent of citrus that rolled off him made me relax even further. Adjusting my apron again, I looked back at him.

"Do you cook or bake? You jumped at my suggestion, and you don't seem to be uncomfortable in the kitchen."

It was true. The moment we stepped into the kitchen, a different, calmer demeanor took over Colby. His eyes flashed with excitement, even though this petite space was far from a gourmet kitchen. With how fast he got his sleeves out of the way and began inspecting the contents of the pot that simmered–which I had to do my best to ignore the chords of his veins that caught my eye and how his hands picked up the spices that lay in a disorderly manner along the counter–he was already deep in thought figuring out what I'd been working on before he finally answered.

"Actually, I do. Not baking really, but I've always loved cooking. It's a secret passion of mine."

Blinking several times at the admission, he circled back around, so lost in thought he forgot how small the area was. Before either of us knew it, he was turned around and knocking into me, pressing my back against the opposite counter, his chest heaving in surprise against mine.

Neither of us moved or dared to speak; our hastened breathing was the only sound. My eyes darted to his, wondering if he'd move. But when he didn't, I found myself feeling electrified by the proximity, the warmth of his bare arms that lightly touched my own, the way he looked at me like I was the best thing to eat in this kitchen. I was so distracted, I didn't realize the intimacy was causing my pulse to zing out of control, and accidentally force my magic to react.

Suddenly, a bag of flour that sat prominently on the shelf above us, fell, making a snow flurry of flour rain down on top of us. In seconds, we were both covered head to toe in flour–a perfectly tension-filled moment ruined by Ginger, the clumsiest Elf on the planet.

9

One Wall Down

Colby

I don't think I remember ever laughing so hard. After a brief moment of the two of us standing there in absolute silence, covered in flour–we both busted out in laughter not able to speak for several minutes. It was the type of laugh that released worries, released pain, and one I wasn't sure I'd experience again.

Hearing the allure of Ginger's laughter, the way she snorted, attempting to catch her breath, was irresistible. When I gave a good effort to brush off the flour, I ended up raising my hands up in defeat–we were completely covered, and Ginger found it ridiculously hilarious.

Talk about pouring flour on a hot moment!

Ginger finally came down from the laughing fit and quirked her eyebrow at me.

"Did I warn you that I was a bit of a mess in the kitchen?"

Her eyes gleamed at me, and I felt a flutter at the sight of those eyes peering through the flour that caked her face, but still–I'd kiss her this way.

"I would've noticed by the way your spices were strewn about like a battlefield, but I think this seals the deal on my assumption of your messy nature, Cupcake."

In my semi-beer induced and laughter roaring episode, I'd forgotten the last time we saw each other, she told me not to call her that nickname, and waited for the defiance and a prompt kicking out again—but her eyes flickered with confusion and then to acceptance, a shyness returning.

Maybe the nickname wasn't so irksome anymore? After all, the nickname was accurate. She was as sweet and tantalizing as a cupcake.

Ginger walked over to a back closet and grabbed a couple of towels, throwing one at me. I used it to wipe my face and hands the best I could. We hadn't even started, and the kitchen was a wreck. Once moderately cleaned up, I went back to the pot on the stove and sniffed again.

"This is potato-leek filling, right? You should really put some thyme in there. It'd give it an earthier flavor."

Her eyebrow shot up in interest.

"You could tell it needed thyme by just smelling it?"

I smiled and shrugged, playing at indifference. "My friend Tom says it's a gift, I have a knack for being able to tell what's in something by the smell. I know, it's a little strange."

Her eyes left mine as she looked around for the small bag of thyme. When she handed it to me, I was genuinely surprised at her instant agreement to my suggestion. I took the package and pulled out enough for a sprinkle, adding it to the pot. Without a word, she handed me a spoon, and I slowly began letting the combination of chopped potatoes, leeks, carrots, celery and spices mix together. She watched me for a while before speaking again; I found the silence didn't bother me—it actually made me feel relaxed being there with her that way.

"It's not weird. If I didn't know any better, I would say your friend is right. That is a gift, and not one many have. I was curious about the cook-off you used to have in your Christmas festival that I read about it in an old pamphlet left in the café. Did you ever participate?"

The mention of the cook-off threw me off, but it was in every pamphlet around town—she was bound to know about the festival. But the sting from the flooding of memories that came with her question, wasn't easily ignored.

"Yeah, years ago my mom pushed me to enter, and on a couple of occasions I did place in the top 3. But we haven't held the Christmas festival in awhile, though, I know everyone misses it. Including myself."

I have no idea why I was admitting this to a complete stranger, but something about Ginger made me crave to. I was feeling incredibly comfortable in her presence, on top of the fact I find myself slack-jawed at the sheer way her eyes flicker to mine, or how I feel this desire to wrap her petite frame into my arms, lift her up, making her toes curl from the wicked things I'd enjoy doing to her.

For a split second, when I'd let my curiosity of her cooking essentials get the better of my focus, and spun to find her right there, pressed against the counter, it took everything in me not to kiss her until she was breathless. Until those cheeks formed the same crimson color of her hair that stuck out frantically, but still made her look more lovely than any woman I'd seen before.

Then that damned flour bag fell at the precise moment I was about to kiss a woman I barely knew; maybe in the end that wasn't meant to be, despite the increasing pull to her. Because I had to be certifiably nuts to fall this fast for someone who I didn't even know. I needed to get a grip, or this could end badly. As it usually did.

Ginger glanced at me from the corner of her eyes as we both worked the pie crust dough with our hands, our elbows knocking occasionally in the dismally small space.

"If you don't mind me asking, why did the Christmas festival stop? It was one of the reasons I moved here. Not sure if you can tell by my apron, but Christmas is my favorite time of the year. I've heard so much about how big you all did it for the Christmas season, the parade, the competitions, the lights and entertainment...so what made it all stop? I don't even see a single wreath up in the square."

I sighed, because she wasn't wrong. It's been so long since anybody in the town has walked around happily during the holidays, and unfortunately, it was all my father's fault. What would happen if I told her the reason? That the loss of my mother wrecked not only my life, but the town's? That my father didn't go to me for comfort, or anybody else, he merely took away the option of celebrating for everybody because it was too painful for him to see the holiday my mother cherished above all others. How each and every year since her passing, the people of Everly Cove were forced to keep their merriment and cheer to the confines of their homes out of respect for my family's mourning. How even though her own mother named her after the town she loved more than any other, and how that love was one of the things he and her bonded over in their time together, he could hardly speak her name without a single shred of evidence of his love for her. What many assumed to be implemented only the first Christmas, my father kept up the ban ever since, causing a deflation in spirits and overall camaraderie of the townspeople.

At last, I decided perhaps it's time to let someone in. Even for a moment. I blamed the couple of beers I had, and Tom's words ringing in my ear about why I shouldn't give up the chance at happiness.

"5 years ago my mother passed away. Early onset Dementia. Christmas happened to be her favorite time of the year, and ever since my father came into office, he made it a priority to celebrate. When my mother's memory waned, most days she found it hard to remember who either one of us was. But at Christmas time, when my dad pulled out all the stops, we realized it was one of the only times she could remember. Her memory would come back, she'd be more interactive and even recall memories from years past. She brightened up and was the happiest during each holiday season. When she passed away, my dad not only didn't grieve her at all, but he pretty much punished the community. He couldn't stand to look at an ornament, or snowman, or any decoration for that matter. He temporarily banned the Christmas festival that year, but each year since, it still hasn't returned."

Not noticing Ginger stopped kneading the dough, I felt a soft hand on my forearm, and now with her delicate fingers on my skin, my heart jolted involuntarily at the contact. In that touch was sincerity, a comfort I didn't feel before when talking about my mother with anyone else. Aunt Annie was kind and loving, but she was also the type of person who rarely lived within her sadness, opting for unabashed optimism instead. But that method didn't seem to work for me, so feeling someone else notice my sadness, but not in a demeaning way, made me realize just how much I needed that sort of connection. Especially considering my dad and I haven't even spoken about my mother together since the day of her funeral.

"Colby, I had no idea. I'm so sorry. I can tell the topic brings up a lot of hurt for you, and I apologize if my prying was out of line. But...what if we restarted the Christmas festival, in your mother's honor? If she adored it so much, we could let it live on as her legacy. I would be more than happy to help set it up with you."

Blinking several times, I waited for the usual bitterness to creep back in, to overwhelm me with this sense of scorned, grieving child syndrome, where everyone around me suffered the wrath of my inability to cope with her death.

It didn't come.

Instead, a renewed feeling of hope replaced that usual frosted interior of my heart—the one I'd repaved like a zamboni for the last several years with fierce tenacity.

I wonder if this was the feeling the Grinch experienced when his heart grew three sizes that day?

All I could feel was overwhelming gratitude to this sweet, red-haired woman who came to this town like a beacon of light and joy, sharing it with everyone she came in contact with. Those tawny eyes made my heart melt entirely, and the delight I felt at the thought of someone helping me reinstate the festival, specifically to honor my mother's memory rather than to erase it; it was more than I could take.

Impulsively, with my chest beating like a trumpet, I pulled Ginger by the waist, not allowing a second longer to pass for my sense to stop me from what I do next. My hand found its way to the back of her neck beneath those tremendous waves, and when she didn't pull away, I leaned closer, our mouths so close to touching, and whispered against them softly.

"Thank you.."

I wondered why I couldn't bring myself to say more. To say how much I felt seen by her. To thank her for acknowledging my feelings, when no one else could see the hurt that sat beneath the surface each and every day. For the way she said sorry with empathy rather than pity. How she didn't know me, and yet she offered to help me achieve something to reconnect with my mother in a healthy way, in a way that could continue on for years to come. Not out of spite for my father's wishes, *but out of redemption for my own.*

But none of these words came, my chest ached and contracted, and despite feeling like I could speak this truth to her, this moment; was only for gratitude. For the quirky, fiery inside and out woman who was slowly giving me space to let down these barriers of strength I built. The ones that kept me from breaking apart altogether. So instead, I kissed her. Hoping that everything that rattled in my head I didn't have the bravery to voice, would come through even just a little bit.

I kissed her like my life depended on it. Maybe it did.

10

Banquet Bombshell

Ginger

Looking in the mirror, I did a twirl, admiring the dress I'd gotten from the consignment shop down the street yesterday–the morning after the incredible kiss Colby landed on me in the shop's kitchen.

After that kiss, neither of us could hardly speak, but the tension between us was hovering in the air, and I could see a smile out of the corner of my eye once we'd placed the pies in the oven. He left with a cordial goodbye, saying the next couple of days would be busy, and we'd see each other again at the dinner tonight for all the local businesses in town. The rest of the evening, I was jumping around like a crazed bee, buzzing about the cottage, talking Gimli's ears off about the kiss, which he promptly reminded me wasn't a big deal and that he didn't understand the concept of humans mashing their mouths together for pleasure.

But the kiss wasn't the only thing I was buzzing about. It was the information I'd gotten from Colby about the reasons the Christmas

Spirit fell away to nothing in the first place: because his mother passed, and his father halted the holiday celebrations.

I had an answer! It was a major lead, and a major hunk who was going to help me figure this out. For the first time in years, I may not have solved the North Pole's energy crisis yet, but I was well on my way to. Now, if we reinstated the Christmas festival, we had a chance at restoring balance here, and hopefully, the Pole. I relayed the news to Izabelle the next day once the morning coffee and breakfast rush ended, and she was impressed with my progress. She asked how I got Colby to open up to me when he acted so churlish at the opening; I said he offered the information rather easily, although I neglected to mention that what followed was the best kiss of my life. I didn't want Izabelle reporting back to my sister that I wasn't remaining professional. Even though he kissed me, not the other way around. I could play it off like that if it came out.

For now, I relished the moment all for myself, because it was honestly priceless. The two of us, covered in flour, baking together in a tiny kitchen, a moment of vulnerability that made me realize how much I too, needed a connection like that–and a kiss that would've knocked my white and red stockings from my North Pole uniform right off if I'd been wearing them! I couldn't help but smile at the memory of his strong arms wrapped around my lower back, and his lips as soft as freshly fallen snow. Izabelle walked behind me while I was in mid-thought and held up two pairs of earrings in front of me.

"I would say the pair on the right matches with the color of your dress, but the left pair to me says *daring*. It all depends on what kind of impression you want to make tonight."

I agreed with her and picked out an emerald green cocktail dress that stopped above my knee. It flowed out elegantly at my waist, and the top part was accentuated by beads of the same color. The earrings that matched would definitely look nice with it, but the pair that Izabelle referred to as *daring* were these golden multi-hoops that drooped down. They would definitely make a statement, and I found myself wondering if Colby would like them.

I took the gold pair out from Izabelle's hand and held it up to my ear.

"I think I'd like to be daring today. I could use the pep since this is so important we get approval to reinstate the festival from Colby's dad."

Plus, I'd like to look so good that Colby can't help but pull me into an empty room at the inn and kiss me like he did the other night.

After putting on the earrings, I face Izabelle, who's wearing a tight fitting, black velvet dress that fell at her knees. A slit was going dangerously high on her thigh, but if anyone could pull it off, it was her. She held a leather jacket over her arm, and her makeup used hints of red today. We definitely looked like total opposites, but over the last few days, with lots of preparation for the customers and coming up with the proposal for the festival, I'd come to see we were similar in a lot of ways.

She had several siblings, one of which she felt was always hovering. We vented for several hours over a couple of spiked hot cocoas the night before about it, and I found extreme comfort in knowing I wasn't the only one with sibling issues. She also was incredibly hardworking, and found that her hobby of playing music and painting was something she always loved. Specifically the electric guitar, which she proceeded to pull out and play, and it was one of the best songs I'd ever heard.

Turns out, everybody yearned for something else, that everyone dealt with hard people and finding their way in the world. Not just me. I ended the night hugging her neck, a little tipsy and a little emotional from venting about my sister, and although I got the sense she wasn't the most touchy-feely person, she hugged me back before leaving my cottage for the night. We were finding a genuine friendship with each other, which is why I invited her back over to get ready for the dinner together.

Putting the earrings on and doing a final look in the mirror, I felt confident in a way I wasn't expecting, and it felt absolutely invigorating! I grabbed my coat, which didn't match my dress at all, and we sprinted out the door together to the cab that was waiting to take us to dinner.

***

We arrived at the Harbor Restaurant & Inn as snow was beginning to fall. It was 5 minutes before the event began at 7pm, and after both Izabelle and I struggled our way through the door with the giant cake box, we were directed to a table to place it on, which sat prominently on the wall that was loaded to the brim with tables containing all l kinds of delicious foods. The event was being done buffet style, and there was a table specifically designated for my cake, apparently Annie herself mentioned it to the manager before arriving. Before even taking off my coat, Izabelle helped me slide the cake box onto the table as I precariously pulled it out, and put it on the cake stand I'd brought. As I stood back to see if it was placed in the center of the table, I couldn't help but hold back a happy squeal.

It was by far the prettiest cake I've ever made! It has 5 tiers, each getting larger as it went further down, covered in glistening white buttercream frosting that I'd made from scratch. Around the edges of each tier were white fondant fir trees neatly placed and intermixed with real cranberries and leaves in a cascading flow all along the cake. On top, was my signature secret recipe gingerbread cookies, shaped like snowflakes, with delicate white icing to make the snowflake designs. They stuck out of the top of the cake like a bouquet, and the contrast of the deep, brown cookie against the white cake, was something to behold.

I felt I could cry looking at it. For the first time in my life, I could display my craft openly, and with pride. Not hide it away, only for family. Not be ashamed of my desire to create with my hands like this. Because this time, I didn't use magic to give me a hand. I did every step solely by myself–and although it was a challenge–it was also the most fun I've ever had baking. To be able to display my talent and my passion for all to see in such a beautiful space that added to the cozy elegance of what I've created, was quite literally a dream come true.

Izabelle put a hand on my arm and cleared her throat. We needed to move to the other location where they were gathering before the dinner started.

I nodded and followed her through the dining hall, finally admiring the beauty of the Harbor Restaurant. It was a spacious area, with large windows overlooking the ocean on one side of the room. In the center, was a gigantic stone fireplace with greenery and candles placed upon a mantle. A warm and welcoming fire had already begun filling the room with an embrace that reminded me of the hearth in my own family's home back at the Pole. On one side of the fireplace was a large tree decorated North Pole quality, lights strung and ornaments hanging with reds, greens, and whites displayed perfectly. A long table that looked to sit about 30 or more people, was placed directly in front of the fireplace, set with charming ornamental plates with poinsettias on them, and matching red napkins.

As I looked out the far windows, I could see the lighthouse that was attached to the restaurant itself, and the snow falling outside as waves crashed below us against the craggy rocks beneath, as the Inn was placed exactly on the edge of a small cliff overlooking the Maine coastline. We were told upon arrival we were free to walk to the lighthouse and go up top if we liked after the dinner, as it was open to the public most times unless weather didn't permit. I wondered how lovely it would be to watch the snow illuminated by the moon, and the light reflecting off the ocean below. I made a mental note to take up the offer of walking there after the dinner finished.

Before entering the other room where a bustle of conversations was taking place, a waiter took my jacket to the coat check-in and handed Izabelle and I each a glass of champagne. When we were inside the room, it looked to be some sort of lounge area for the Inn, with leather sofas and high back armchairs, many of which were occupied. I recognized the owner of the consignment store where I shopped from sitting in one, her name was Norma, and she was incredibly helpful in finding the dress for me. I hate to admit I got a little nervous while shopping, but when she went to the back and pulled out this particular dress, my jaw dropped. She looked my way, gave a small wave and a thumbs up, approving of the dress in person. I smiled back, raising my glass to her.

The people of Everly Cove were slowly making their way to a very special place in my heart. The kindness and generosity of each person I'd met so far was making me feel so at home here, which helped with the slight home-sickness I was feeling. And it was making me feel less scared at finding the solution to the most dire problem: increasing Christmas Spirit in Everly Cove. When Norma raised her glass in response and turned her attention to the front of the room, my gaze followed, and I got a glimpse of the top of Colby's curled, brown hair beyond the many heads that stood in front of me, and my heart began to pound.

We'd not seen each other since the night of the kiss, and I was starting to get nervous to see him again. I did my best to stand up straighter and adjusted the sleeves of my dress that ruffled out over my shoulders. All at once, the confidence I felt standing before the mirror faded. When Colby met my eyes, I smiled broadly at him, but he did not share the same reaction. Instead, his eyes darted awkwardly in the opposite direction as I moved closer–*why?*

With one arm linked around his elbow, and a stylish, slicked back bun of bright blonde hair, a woman wearing a short navy dress paired with dangerously high heels–Colby stood at the front of the group next to his father, the woman touching him like they were together. *Intimately* together. And it took everything in me not to drop my champagne.

11

Speeches Turned Spoiled

Colby

If there was somewhere I could hide, I'd run for it right now. When Ginger and I locked eyes from across the room, and she noticed my ex-girlfriend Emma draped on my arm, the change in excitement to see me was instantly replaced with shock, and sadness. Those beautiful hazel irises reflected the same sadness I felt, because the connection that was starting to grow the other night between us, was not something I wished to throw away, but one I wanted to explore.

When Tom heard I'd kissed her, he patted himself on the back and claimed that he was a top notch matchmaker, jokingly wondering if he should make it a full time business. The next couple of days were filled with errands for my dad to ensure the reservation at the Harbor Restaurant for the Business Christmas Banquet, finalize the menu for the buffet, and of course take Zeus to the dog park for some much needed quality time with him. He'd been acting down, and I wanted to make sure I didn't neglect him or our time together. I got him right before my mother passed, and he's been my best and most comforting companion. My day job tended to keep me so busy though, so I found a way to sneak out earlier the afternoon before, and we spent the whole afternoon playing catch as I daydreamed about kissing those peppermint lips of Ginger's again.

When I arrived back just before the end of the work day to let my dad know I'd finished the tasks for the dinner, I dropped the stack of papers and mail I was holding the moment I opened his office door. Sitting on the edge of his desk was Emma. The girl I dated for over a year, who I hadn't seen in 2 years. We dated for awhile, but I always felt like the relationship was more about her than us. She expected me to provide for her, take her out on lavish dates, and tended to get more caught up in celebrity gossip and fashion trends than anything else. She wasn't the fondest of being stuck in a small town like Everly Cove, but the prospect of being a mayor's wife was what enticed her the most. No matter how much I told her it was never my wish to follow in my dad's footsteps, she insisted my mind would change when I got more past my grief and more used to having a gorgeous girl like her on my arm permanently. It was a relationship that pleased my dad, and although we had our good moments, I felt like it was always surface level. There wasn't true love or deep conversations, and it only ever felt like a way to pass time as I tried to work through my feelings. The company was nice, sure, and she was beautiful–but I always knew I craved more than that. And she knew it too. When she was offered a position at a law firm in San Diego, California, she hopped on a plane so fast, our breakup was only a few lines of text.

I hadn't seen or spoken to her since, until she was suddenly running to hug me as though that text message never happened and she hadn't trash talked Everly Cove and wanted to get as far away from it as possible. When my dad declared she'd be staying for the remainder of the holiday, per his invitation, my anger bubbled to the surface, but I wouldn't let either of them know. Jackson's didn't have outbursts. We held our pain close, and our anger even closer. We were too much the face of the town to ever be anything else.

I slapped on a ridiculous smile for the vain snake I thought I'd never see again, and to my surprise, Emma seemed to change. She immediately hugged me and apologized for how she left. She professed she should've had a proper break up face-to-face, rather than a text message. I was so stunned, as I never thought she'd apologize for a single thing in her life, and hugged her back. Her and dad made arrangements to meet together at the dinner, which he'd invited her to, and the rest is what was happening as we speak.

Emma clinging to my arm. Ginger across the room seeing it all. And I was inexplicably dumbstruck as to how I got into this mess. On the way to dinner, my father drummed into me how much of a successful and lovely girl Emma had become, even more so than she was before. How she'd make a fine Jackson woman, and that I needed to start thinking seriously about my future. All I could do was white knuckle the steering wheel and breathe as his relentless opinions rendered me silent and obedient.

How in God's name am I thirty-two years old and I can't tell this man, no, damnit!

Because although we didn't get along, he was all I had other than my Aunt Annie. The last thread connected to my mother and the childhood we had together. Despite our differences in opinions on career, Theo Jackson has been an incredible dad, and until his schedule became riddled with mayoral duties, he was a steady influence in my life. A comfort. Even though it'd been years since it was like that together, I grasped that memory of him tightly. I couldn't lose him, either. No matter how hard it'd become between us since my mother's death. I always feared in the back of my mind that if I told him straight up "no", that somehow that was interconnected to saying no to my future relationship with him altogether. So with steady practice, I learned how to bottle those feelings up tightly, and toss that bottle out to the Gulf of Maine.

Seeing Ginger now though, this way, was making me wish past me had told both my dad and Emma to leave me alone. I didn't know the repercussions it'd have, or how hurt Ginger would look seeing us together, especially after the other night. And damn, if that wasn't a kiss I'd thought about over and over since then. My father's nagging voice wouldn't leave me alone though, and something about Emma struck me as different, something I wasn't quite sure I could place.

What if the old man was right and it was time I found a wife?

It's not like Emma wasn't gorgeous, but ever since I saw those hazel eyes and red curls, Ginger had ensnared my mind almost entirely since arriving in town. I was becoming more confused with each minute, and I was too much of a coward to look at Ginger right now. The sadness in those eyes would break me.

Luckily, everyone's attention went to my dad as he raised a champagne glass up high. I felt Emma tighten her grip on my arm, and I shuffled in place uncomfortably.

"Welcome, friends! I'm so glad you could all join us for our 10th annual Business Christmas Banquet!"

Applause scattered around the room, and I kept my attention on my clapping hands to avoid catching Ginger's gaze.

"Each year, we come together as entrepreneurs to talk about our great town of Everly Cove and how we can better ourselves as a community. What makes Everly Cove so special, is the harmony we have amongst our neighbors, our friends, and how we work together to leave a legacy that no one is soon to forget. Now before we begin dinner, it's customary to have presentations from our leading business owners for new ideas to move us forward in the New Year."

My father's secretary, Cathy, a young woman just out of high school, incredibly peppy–almost annoyingly so–was eager to participate in any town events and volunteered happily to assist at the dinner tonight. Walking up to dad with a clipboard, she handed it to him, and thanked her before clearing his throat and scanning the page on it.

"Looks like first up we have Ginger Tinsel, our new café owner, and.." he paused for a moment and raised his eyebrows in surprise, "and..my son, Colby Jackson?"

Damn! I forgot all about the presentation for renewing the Christmas festival with Ginger.

After the kiss the night before, and all the hectic mess of getting the final details for the dinner figured out, I'd totally forgotten I'd agreed to do the presentation *with* her before I left. My father looked at me quizzically, and I felt Emma's eyes bore into me intensely from my side. I coughed and walked closer to my dad, who handed me a microphone as I waited for Ginger to come forward. When I saw her small figure step between bodies, revealing herself, I felt like an absolute idiot. She looked stunning. Wearing a green dress that accentuated her curves, the color made her fiery hair pop even more than usual, and the glow of her eyes flashed brightly from the light hanging overhead; instantly, I licked my lips, wondering if she was wearing that same peppermint lip gloss as before.

Her cheeks flushed red, and she held her hands awkwardly in front of her as she walked to stand beside me, not a hello or anything, and my stomach dropped.

I did my best to not stare too long, and cleared my throat again, putting the microphone closer, which elicited a screeching sound that made everybody cover their ears.

"Ah, sorry...sorry. Um...so Ginger and I are here to discuss a new proposal, not for the New Year, but for this year."

I paused, but my lackluster public speaking skills were not doing anyone, especially myself, any favors. Not to mention, I didn't have anything prepared to help Ginger on the presentation at all. When silence carried on for far too long and with zero ideas popping in my head, not to mention the look of disapproval my dad was giving me, I went totally frozen. Ginger apparently noticed, gently taking the microphone from my hand.

How much worse could this get?

"Uh...yes, everybody, like Colby was saying–our proposal is for reinstating the Christmas festival, starting the first of next week, actually."

The entire room erupted into murmurs, and I panicked at agreeing to do such a thing so blatantly in front of my dad, who specifically ended the Christmas festivities due to *his* grief. I dared not look in his direction as Ginger continued on, as I stood there like a deer caught in headlights.

"Our plan is to bring back some holiday joy this year, by getting the Christmas festival set up again! The proposal would be to start next week–I know it's not a lot of time, as Christmas is now only a couple weeks away, but I promise, I've gotten all the details figured out. Monday, we will start with a Christmas Tree farm in the square, along with games, baking competitions..." Ginger's eyes flicked over to me momentarily when she said the last bit, "Food vendors, and crafts." She paused and took a deep breath before continuing. "The following week, we will finish on Christmas Eve with a ball, a dance if you will... in honor of Everly Jackson herself, as a fundraiser for the Maine Chapter of the National Foundation for Dementia."

My heart was hammering against my chest so fast, and when I saw Emma made her way to my dad's side, patting his back in a comforting manner, his stern expression more severe than ever–with a hint of betrayal in his eyes–I wasn't sure if I was going to pass out or barf in front of everyone.

Suddenly, when I thought boos would ensue, a fierce applause broke out, and shock was all I could feel. Whooping noises came from the left corner, a whistle from the right, everybody elated at the idea of bringing back the festival. Ginger clapped along with everybody else, flashing one of the biggest smiles in the room. Without consulting my dad, his secretary called out a show of hands in favor of the proposal, and every hand in the room shot up; except my dad's. And I couldn't help but feel guilty. I watched as he whispered something to Emma, and they both walked out of the room together without another word to anyone.

Ginger handed the microphone back to Cathy, and I silently followed her as she shook hands, took congratulations, and was told how brilliant it would be to have the joy of the past years again for this season. When we finally got to the back of the crowd, and the next presentation began, I stood next to Ginger. She crossed her arms, doing her best to not look at me. As the owner from the nearby fish market began his speech, I tried to fill the gap of the agonizing silence between us.

"You spoke great...I think your plan for the festival will be amazing."

Ginger rolled her eyes and turned to me, angrier than I'd seen even at the café opening when she told me to not hit the door on the way out. Her voice was a hushed, angry whisper.

"Glad I got your stamp of approval, Colby. Would've appreciated to know in advance that you were going to leave me hanging up there. Or that you were bringing a date with you." She paused and lowered her voice even further. "I was under the impression we'd be meeting here together."

Her voice was tinged with an unfulfilled hope, and possibly regret. Which made me feel sick to my stomach. How could I possibly explain the pressure I'm under with my dad to her? Would she ever understand that a Jackson was first obligated to his duty, over his desires? That my father was the last true connection to my mother, and how I couldn't bear to lose him too? I stumbled over my next words.

"Look...Ginger...I'm so sorry. For both. I never intentionally wanted to hurt you."

Vague, but true. Yet I could see the hurt painted all over her beautiful freckled face, her eyes scanning mine for truth.

"You know, when you opened up to me the other night, I thought you were taking the proposal seriously. For your mother's sake. I suggested it...to...help. To bring comfort to you and everybody else in this town. I didn't know that it was all fake."

She grabbed a glass off the nearby tray of a waiter passing by, and stormed out of the room in the same direction as my father and Emma. I stood totally dumbfounded when I heard a familiar cough behind me. Before bracing myself to face her wrath, I downed my champagne like water, and turned to face my aunt, whose eyes were burrowing holes into me like I'd been seized by a demon.

"Colby Renee Jackson, what on God's green Earth are you thinking?"

Annie wore a sequin, purple dress that hung in fringes at the bottom. Wrapping her shoulders in a black shawl, her hair was in braids plaited in a bun formation on the top of her head, several pieces hanging down precisely by her deep, brown eyes—the ones that reminded me so much of my own mother. Her hands were on her hips, and she was tapping a foot impatiently, the way she always did when I misbehaved as a child.

"Hi Auntie, nice seeing you tonight."

She pulled me by my wrist, and walked me towards the wall, away from prying ears. When she released me, I rubbed my wrist.

"Ouch. What are you doing?"

"What do you think I'm doing? I'm scolding you like the idiot you are."

I shrugged my shoulders and looked around in hopes of finding another waiter coming by.

"Yeah I know, dad is going to kill me for being a part of restarting the festival."

Raising an eyebrow at me like I'd just slapped her, she spoke again in hushed tones.

"Now boy, you know that's not at all what I'm referring to. I think it's the best thing to happen in years bringing the festival back to life–I'm talking about why you have that wretched girl hooked around your arm and why I just saw Ginger bolting for the door."

Her words forced me to look her way, the thought of what I'd done was eating away at me. How could I have let this happen? Even my aunt knew how wrong it was to let that woman crawl back into my life.

"I know…Dad invited her and I…you know how hard it is for me to say no to him. She apologized, and has been very kind since she arrived. I just thought if I gave it a try…"

"Give it a try? You mean break apart the one good relationship I've seen you have in years?"

My words stuttered in my mouth.

"Relationship? What do you mean? Ginger and I aren't togethe–"

"Oh shush, you fool. I may be getting older, but if you think I'm too dumb to notice how you two stare at each other, the tension I felt between you two at the opening–you are cute, nephew, but even you can't be that daft. There's something between you, and you're about to throw it away for Emma, a girl who never wanted to see you for who you are."

Above all else, my aunt was always right. Annoyingly so—but right nonetheless. She had a knack for knowing when people were good for each other, knowing when something else was brewing under the surface, and in all my life, I've never known her to get it wrong when she had a hunch about something–or *someone.* I wondered for many years if she was psychic, but whether it was messages from the beyond or something else, Aunt Annie knew me better than anyone else, even more than myself these days.

"Yeah, well...I may have screwed it up. How could I possibly fix it now? Or even know what I want, or who, for that matter?"

She saw the desperation in my tone and reluctantly put down her anger for affection, rubbing my arm comfortingly.

"Child, you are lost. But that doesn't mean you don't know what's not good for you. Emma only ever brought you heartache. Perhaps there's a reason she's here–a role for her to play–but, do you really think she's here for good intentions?"

Sighing, I rubbed my temples, a headache emerging, and looked into her eyes.

"No, probably not. But you saw what an idiot I was up there, Annie. How could I possibly fix this?"

"Well, for one, you could go find Ginger and apologize. Tell her where your heart lies. Because I know for a fact, it doesn't lie with the past."

"Yes...I think you're right, Auntie."

Aunt Annie laughed heartily, slapping my arm playfully.

"Colby, when am I not?"

I rolled my eyes at her sheer belief in herself and remembered her comment from earlier.

"You said she ran out of here? Do you know where?"

"She was hanging around the other side of the hall, I bet she isn't far. Go! I'll man the fort here and keep an eye out for Emma and your father."

Smirking at her insult, I kissed her cheek and began scanning the crowd, looking for the exit to the hallway. Annie's words gave me not only the wake-up call I needed, but a call to action. I needed to find Ginger as quickly as possible. I needed to find a way to fix this—before it's too late.

12

Merry Mistep

Ginger

I should be celebrating. The reaction to the Christmas festival was a roaring success. But here I was, heading towards the dining room, chugging a glass of champagne, alone.

The sting from Colby's lack of care in helping me with the presentation, on top of the fact he brought a date to the function, was making me question what happened between us in the first place. Because even though I was here for work, to literally save Christmas, I'd started to fall for him. The kiss only solidified the attraction I felt towards him since the post office that day—even if he infuriated me beyond belief.

I was getting in way over my head, and no matter how much progress I was making on my mission, my heart felt like it was shattering into a million pieces tonight. As I rounded the corner of the hallway leading back towards the dining room, figuring I'd check on my cake and snap some shots to remember it by, I slowed my pace when I saw the blonde girl who'd been hanging on Colby's arm before the presentation, and his father. They stood huddled together, Colby's father clearly furious, and the girl was attempting to calm him down.

I hesitated if I should turn back around, but when she looked up to find me standing there, her crystal blue eyes recognizing me, she whispered something to Colby's dad, who turned to me.

There's still half a glass of champagne. Would it be too obvious that I'm nervous to speak to Colby's dad if I downed the rest before getting the nerve to boldly walk up to him?

Colby's dad made a shushing motion to the woman, who crossed her arms indignantly. He then straightened his suit jacket and walked towards me. He put on a devilish smile, shooting a hand out for me to shake.

"Ginger! What a wonderfully presented proposal, my dear. How thoughtful it was to think of my wife in such a dignified and noble way. This is Emma Carlisle, an old friend of the family."

I glanced at the girl over his shoulder, who stood judgingly behind him, she gave a small nod, but not a single word out of her mouth for a greeting. An icky feeling filled my body remembering her latched to Colby's arm.

Friend? She seemed more than friendly with him.

"Sir, it's a pleasure to meet you both. Thank you for the compliment. In all honesty, it was my suggestion, but once I mentioned it to your son, he was the one to come up with such wonderful events in her honor. Including the ball."

Mr. Jackson raised an eyebrow. "Not so much. A compliment comes when you've earned it. Colby? I wasn't aware you two were so acquainted. Nor that he even knew how to dance."

I stifled a chuckle. The image of Colby in a black suit and tie, glasses slipping down his nose, trying to figure out the steps at a ball, was something I hoped I'd be seeing myself as the one who was doing her best to avoid getting her feet stepped on by him. As his partner at the ball. But clearly, after tonight, that wouldn't be the case. The double meaning in Mr. Jackson's words made me get snowflakes in my stomach. If he had any idea what actually transpired between us or not, I didn't know. But the way his somber expression, and how the girl was standing behind him like a bouncer at a club, I had the bad feeling he had a suspicion.

"Umm...well we spoke a bit after the café opening, and when he told me about his mother, and about how tremendous your town's Christmas festivals used to be, I couldn't help wondering how glorious it might be to see that happen again, and for a good cause. He's incredibly fond of her, and you, Sir."

Mr. Jackson didn't respond for a moment, merely picking at a finger on his hand and sighing.

"My wife was so dear to not only my family, but this town. But, because of the festive holiday being her favorite, her memory lingered during each subsequent season in a way that made my heart wrench in longing for her. This is why I stopped the festival. Yet as I see here tonight, apparently to the detriment of my constituents. I look forward to seeing how you, *and* Colby, honor my wife this Christmas season." His words were friendly, many would even say encouraging–but the tone gave it away–Mr. Jackson wasn't at all happy with what I was doing.

With a curt nod, he turned away, and the girl gave a final glare at me before leaving with him. They found seats at the head of the dining table, waiting for the remainder of the presentations to finish. I felt tears stinging the corners of my eyes. So I finished the rest of my champagne, and rushed to the exit leading to the lighthouse. There was no way I could face them at a long dinner right now when my courage was all but gone, and my heart felt like stomped snow.

Stepping outside, the frigid air came as a welcome relief. I was burning up from confusion, frustration, and just straight embarrassment–it felt like my skin was going to burn through the fabric of the emerald dress. Snowfall began as the clicking of my heels echoed in the empty pathway heading to the entrance of the lighthouse.

Standing bold in traditional red and white stripes, its giant beam of light reveals where the crashing waves meet the jagged rocks beneath. I hugged myself to steady my breathing, my thoughts rapidly approaching reindeer-level speeds.

How could I have gotten involved like this?

Not only had I risked the exposure of my world and the very success of this mission–I let my Elf heart get the better of me. Now I was stuck in a ridiculous love triangle with a woman who could trump me in the beauty department on her worst day, and with a man who quite literally seemed to be hot one second, and colder than the Pole, the next. Instead of making Everly Cove better, it was becoming blaringly clear that I may well be making myself an enemy here.

The sneering glare from Mr. Jackson and the pressure to honor Mrs. Jackson, made it seem like I had spit in his cocoa and served it to him. Her judgment beside him with a knowing look she enjoyed seeing me defeated. Oh, and Colby leaving me high and dry on the presentation without so much as making eye contact with me? All of it painted a rich tapestry of one of the worst nights of my life, when I thought it might've been one of the best.

And above all that, even though I desperately wanted to give way to unleashing a storm of my own, my magic humming in anticipation as my emotions swirled inside me, the main thing on my mind was this: that I stupidly believed that kiss with Colby actually meant something.

The worst part? I hoped it had. I even believed it meant he wanted to come to this event *with* me. Like a *date*. Instead, I arrived after spending an hour getting myself ready in a way I never have before, to find him with someone else. The Colby who shifted before my eyes, baking with me, the one who became vulnerable speaking of his mother, the one who kissed me as if he'd just come up for air after years of drowning–that Colby was not the one I saw tonight.

We weren't anything. He wasn't my boyfriend. He wasn't even supposed to *be* someone I wanted. Everything about this was unallowed by centuries of tradition and rules. So why was I feeling an anger that rivaled the Snow Yetis beyond our village for a man who made me feel this badly?

That's it. No more unnecessary attachments. Colby Jackson isn't worth the end of my career or the success of this mission. He isn't worth me. There are clearly two Colbys—and I want nothing to do with either. I refuse to fall for him.

The path curved around a steep embankment, the winter wind clawing at my coat as my anger twisted up tighter and tighter inside me. Sparks bled from my fingertips, little bursts of silver-white and red snapping in the air. I shoved my hands under my arms to smother them, but the magic pulsed against my skin, straining to break free. Tears stung at the corners of my eyes. I squeezed them shut, blinking hard, refusing to let them spill. I wouldn't cry. I wouldn't crack. I wouldn't fall—

Then the ground vanished beneath my foot. And despite every protest, I fell anyway.

13

Ho, Ho, Help!

Colby

I 'd already done a lap around the room twice in search of Ginger. She was clearly upset, and she had every right to be. My actions have been so wrong by her, especially with showing up with Emma the way I did. I twisted my hands together impatiently. Finally frustrated, I scurried my way past the crowd and made a beeline to the dining hall, my aunt's words haunting my every step. The dinner portion of the evening was beginning, and if she were to be anywhere, it would be here—to present the cake she made for the event.

I stood impatiently by the table, in hopes she was in the bathroom and would be coming to sit down any minute. If I could wave her over, maybe during the bustle of dinner, I could apologize again, and make sure she was aware that Emma's arrival wasn't planned. I spotted a seat next to Izabelle, the girl Ginger hired as the manager for the café, who I didn't notice was already seated at the other end. Her black hair fell in waves down her shoulders, and her dark eyeliner made it hard to see her brown eyes that watched me tentatively as I made my way towards her, taking the chair next to her.

Izabelle eyed me up and down but kept quiet, as the others were now making their way from the lounge room and finding seats. It had only been a few minutes since Annie saw Ginger, but after almost every seat was filled, I anxiously looked around for Ginger, but I couldn't find her anywhere. When I noticed Izabelle was doing the same thing, I leaned over and whispered to her.

"Where's Ginger?"

Izabelle didn't look at me; instead, she continued scanning the crowd and the doorway.

"I have no clue. I saw her rush out of the room after the presentation, but when I followed into the hallway, she wasn't there. I decided to wait here, but I don't see her."

Did she leave because of how much of an idiot I was?

The table was completely filled, each seat claimed, except the one next to me. *Where Ginger should've been.* Izabelle was now visibly stiff, her expression changing from nonchalant coolness to concern. She whispered to me again.

"Something's wrong. She should be here to present the cake."

"Yes, I know she was asked to make one by Annie."

Izabelle crossed her arms. "Yes, and I know she wouldn't miss it unless something was very wrong."

I looked around the room again and met the eyes of my father, eyes narrowed in my direction as he frowned at me in a way different, and harsher than usual. I couldn't let him distract me right now. If Izabelle was saying it was unlike Ginger to not be here for this moment, then I think I messed up more than I could've imagined. I stood quickly and went across the room to the maître d', who stood behind a podium, shushing waiters and waitresses, ready to assist at the beginning of the buffet dinner. When I arrived at the podium, I knocked on the wood impatiently. The man turned to me, his voice polite.

"Yes sir, how may I help you?"

"Uhhhh yes, um, you didn't happen to see a girl with red hair in the hallway earlier, did you?"

The gentleman nodded, and I breathed a sigh of relief.

"Yes, I saw her heading towards the lighthouse. Although, I mentioned to a staff member moments ago to go and fetch her, as the snow is picking up outside quite terribly." He looked around and eyed a teenage boy behind him with a mop of sandy blonde hair.

"Jeffrey! Did you go and get the young lady like I asked you?"

The boy looked terrified. "No sir. I'm sorry, I forgot. Chef Pascal said the appetizers were ready and told me to set them out. I didn't remember to go after that."

My mouth fell open, and before either of them could say another word, I sprinted out of the dining hall and towards the same exit heading to the lighthouse. When I opened the door, the wind from earlier had picked up to a hazardous speed; seeing in front of me was becoming harder, no matter how much I attempted to cover my eyes from the snow. Although the lighthouse was technically connected to the Inn, the only visitor access was a pathway that led outside to the main entrance, along the rocky cliff. In daylight, there was plenty of space to navigate the terrain, even in snow. But in these weather conditions, it was treacherous even for a native Mainer, like myself. For an outsider like Ginger, *it was a downright death wish.*

I pulled out my cell phone from my pocket and attempted to use the flashlight to help me see the steps. The light helped, but the wind was getting wilder by the minute. The waves below me are crashing furiously against the shore, so much so, I can feel the mist from the water slightly as I continue to walk. I put an arm over my glasses to try and brace against the snow that was beginning to blister my cheeks and chap my lips, but it was no use. This was a snowstorm from Hell, and Ginger was trapped in it somewhere.

I call out as loudly as I can, snow and wind whipping around my face, and I'd neglected my jacket back at the Inn in an effort to get to Ginger as fast as I could, but the cold was beginning to make me shiver.

"Ginger!! Ginger! Can you hear me?"

I stopped in my tracks and listened, hoping, praying, I'd hear her sweet voice over the sound of waves and wind. When the sound of my heart that seemed to slam against my chest also made it nearly impossible to hear anything, I breathed a sigh of relief when I heard her voice.

"Colby?? I'm over here!"

Her voice echoed up from the darkness, but she was nowhere in sight. Dread hollowed my chest as the truth sank in—she had already fallen.

"**GINGER!**"

I tried to walk quicker, but I didn't know if there was more ice, and I couldn't risk falling down after her. Luckily, when I reached where she fell, I found her only a couple feet down, her hands gripping a large rock. But the panic on her face matched my own; she was panting, trying her best to hold herself up, but the waves below were hitting the side of the cliff so hard, it was shaking the rock she was holding onto.

"Hey, it's okay. Stay calm, Ginger. I'm going to lean down and pull you up. Just don't look down."

"I swear, Colby, if you drop me, I'm going to come back as one of the ghosts from Christmas and haunt you forever!"

If this wasn't a life or death situation, I think I would've rolled my eyes. But banter aside, Ginger was in a seriously dangerous situation. I needed to be quick about this. I looked around myself to see if there was anything I could hold onto, but the pathway was clear, a few stones lining along it towards the lighthouse. So I decided there was no more time to think, I lay down on my belly and leaned as far over the edge as I could stand.

"Ginger, try to reach a hand out!"

Ginger was incredibly focused, trying to get a foot in a better position beneath her, before letting go of one hand and reaching it towards me. We both strained, but we were still a good several inches away, and I had nothing to close the gap. Grunting, I let my body slip a little more, but when gravel began rolling down alongside me and dropping into the sea below, I knew I couldn't get any further to reach her. Ginger yelled up at me, a playfulness tinged in the midst of panic.

"Colby, you are NOT a good rescuer."

I stifled a laugh, continuing to reach out to her, our fingertips almost brushing, but it wasn't enough.

"Look, you were the smart one to walk out here in the middle of a snow storm, Cupcake. Don't think criticizing my rescuing skills helps the situation much."

Ginger's hazel eyes blinked back tears, and I was starting to wonder if I'd have time to rush back inside for help, but the longer she held there, the more her fingers turned a bright red. She was struggling, and it was only a matter of time before her hands gave out. She huffed frustratingly and closed her eyes.

"Alright, alright! I get it! I can get up, but you can't freak out, Colby. Seriously, just don't say a word until we're alone again and safe. Got it?"

"Ginger, what the hell are you talking about?"

Before I could figure out the absurd words she said, the hand Ginger was attempting to use to grab mine, began making light.

Is she lighting a match??

The light turned a bright red and swirled ***out of her hand***! The red swirl began encircling her body, and before my very eyes, she lifted into the air. She literally *flew*. Ginger lifted higher and higher, that swirling light spinning around her, until it gently placed her behind me. I lifted myself up and backed away from the edge.

I opened my mouth to say something but Ginger shushed me.

"Not. A. Word. Can we please, please just go?"

I nodded, my words having totally escaped me at the scene I just witnessed. Silently, I went to wrap my arms around her shoulders, leading her away from the path and to the only place I could think of: away from prying eyes where we could have a much needed conversation. Because it may very well be that Ginger is in fact, a ghost of Christmas something–because I just watched her fly in a Maine snow storm after dangling off a cliff.

14

Mistakes and Mischief

Ginger

I sat on Colby's gray sofa beside Zeus, who was doing his best to warm me up after the incident outside the lighthouse. I already had 2 blankets on, and Zeus' head laid on my lap as I pet his large ears. Although, being an Elf rarely made it so I got cold, hanging from a cliff in the middle of a snowstorm had done me over, and I welcomed Zeus' warm, fluffy body cuddling mine.

The drive in Colby's car was riddled with silence on the way here, and I did my best to calm myself about having exposed my magic to a human. Flying magic wasn't common, as it was only something reindeer and Santa's sled were allowed to use. It was too much of a liability to let Elves fly themselves around willy-nilly all the time; can you imagine the HR headache? But every agent was given a small amount of the magical powder called **Ho-Ho-Hover Dust**, in case of emergencies. And me nearly falling to my demise on the side of a cliff in Maine, and the prospect of freezing in the icy ocean below, yeah, that was enough of an emergency to use it.

Unfortunately, it had to be done in front of human eyes, and that was a clear violation of my protocols.

The Cocoa-mpromise Clause-Subsection B, Paragraph 1

Never under any circumstances let a human know you are an Elf. Never under any circumstances perform magic in front of a human. And above all else, if both of these instances occur, you must report back to HQ immediately so damage control can be initiated. Damage control procedure includes a task force coming to your location, and erasing the memory of the compromised human, so that the integrity of Christmas and the secret of Santa, may be saved.

Note: If any Elf goes against these protocols, they will be released from duty immediately and permanently.

It was taking everything in me to not panic. I'd allowed both things to happen, on my very first mission. A mission that was also the very mission that could make or break Christmas this year. With Christmas Spirit levels plummeting, and Everly Cove having been one of the main places we received that energy from, in recent years, Christmas has barely made it off the ground–literally.

And now on top of that crisis, my entire future as an Elf was at stake. I didn't know if I could call the task force and let them erase Colby's memory. Not only would it erase every bit of progress he has seemed to make with his grief, as he was so eager to restart the festival in his mother's honor, but he'd also lose all memory of me. It'd be like I never existed, I'd be shipped back to the Pole to who knows what, and I'd never see Colby again: a thought that made me fear what it truly meant–that I was beginning to care for Colby in a way I was never supposed to.

Zeus lifted his head when a clanging noise came from the kitchen where Colby was making us coffee. When he stumbled in, holding two large cups of coffee, his dark-brown hair was curling even more than usual after being out in the snow and wind. His glasses were a bit fogged from the steam that came up in plumes from the mugs, as he sat down opposite me after handing me one of them; I smelled a hint of peppermint. Sitting with his own cup, he crossed a leg, having already changed his shirt into a basic henley, but remaining in the black slacks and dress shoes he'd worn to the dinner. I remained in my green dress, but Colby gave me a pair of fuzzy socks to help warm my feet when he checked me for scrapes or bruises, bandaging a few fingers that had been cut from the jagged rocks. Kneading dough for the café the next week would be harder than usual.

I think the café is the least of your worries, Ginger.

I waited for Colby to break the silence, but he sat looking down at the cup in his lap, the cogs in his brain whirring at break-neck speeds from the looks of it. When he gave me the socks, I'd briefly explained what I was. That I was indeed a Christmas Elf. I'd been sent to Everly Cove on a mission to save the holiday spirit here so Christmas in the North Pole would endure. That I'd posed as the new café owner to learn intel on what was causing the Spirit levels to drop so drastically over the last years. The whole time I told my story, Colby didn't say a word. He said a few "mhmms" and all the while, sat silently. When I finished, he declared he'd be going to the kitchen for coffee, and I was left to sit wondering if, while he was doing that, he'd call the police and report a crazy lunatic spouting stuff about Elves and magic and the end of Christmas as we know it.

Taking a small sip of my coffee, it was absolutely delicious, the peppermint seeming to give me an energy boost I didn't realize I so desperately needed. I fidgeted with the mug, wondering what would happen next. Colby hadn't yet said a word in response to my tale, and for some reason, that was scarier than if he'd called me insane.

At last, Colby sighed, removing his glasses to sit on the arm of the chair, rubbing his eyes; he looked exhausted and stressed. When he spoke, my heart stopped entirely.

"If I didn't see you fly with my own eyes, I'd say I was dreaming."

I shifted nervously and took another sip of my coffee, allowing it to warm me from the inside as I nodded in response.

"Yes...if I wasn't in such a dangerous situation, I would've never compromised myself with you."

Colby finally took a swig of his coffee.

"You're not supposed to tell anyone?"

I rubbed Zeus' head to calm my escalating nerves.

"No, never."

Colby raised an eyebrow at me.

"Are there consequences for that?"

My breath caught in the back of my throat, tears waiting impatiently to release, my stomach feeling like it was tied in knots. The consequences of my actions were severe and life-changing–and not just for me. But I couldn't let him know that part.

"Yes, there are. Although...the details on punishment are a bit unclear."

A lie. Doing it made me feel sick. Lying to him didn't feel right, but I wasn't sure if the truth would be any better. How do you tell someone their memory of you needs to be erased? I finally looked up to meet Colby's eyes, that honeyed gaze the most perfect thing I've ever seen.

"But it looks like we've both been untruthful."

Colby looked unsettled at the news of punishment, his hand gripping his cup harder, frustration lacing his next words, obviously confused by my statement.

"Untruthful? What are you talking about?"

I fidgeted with the blanket around my shoulders, trying to calm my senses, but my feelings were raging, they were relentless. They needed release.

"What happened to the Colby from a few nights ago? The one who opened up to me about his grief? The one who made up to me after being a Grinch earlier at the opening? What happened to the Colby who kissed me like it was a breath of fresh air? The one who made me feel safe. Because tonight? That Colby was nowhere to be found. And I am beginning to wonder if you even know which Colby is the real one."

Colby's fists clenched on his lap.

"So you're saying what I said to you wasn't real? That my pain wasn't real?"

This was getting out of control, I wasn't saying it right and both of us were frustrated beyond logic.

"No, no of course not! I believe that was real. But what about us? What about that kiss? Or was I just imagining you being so into me?"

I watched as he thought hard about my question.

"I haven't kissed another woman in two years! Do you think I'd fake that?"

I scoffed. So enraged I couldn't bring myself to speak.

Colby's eyes bulged out at my reaction. Clearly, we both believed something different than what might've been true, but I didn't care, the tensions rising in my body retaliated as he did.

"You know we're getting off the main point here. Why the hell were you out in the snow like that tonight?"

I was taken aback by his tone. It shifted to something along the lines of protective, but anger came through more than anything else.

"I needed...space. I'm not sure I need to explain that to you though, Colby."

Colby's eyes widened in disbelief. I just told him who I was, and not a single remark. But he comes at me displeased because I tried going to the lighthouse alone? My insides boiled at the audacity. He didn't care about me, or about what I might face now that a human knows about me. All he wanted to do was chastise me like a child. He placed his mug on the glass coffee table in front of him so forcefully, I was afraid he'd cracked it.

"Nobody goes running out in a snowstorm along a fucking cliffside, Ginger. At night no less! Have you lost your mind? What would possibly compel you to be so reckless?"

Your nosy, condescending father, you prick.

"That's none of your business. You don't owe me any favors. So thank you for coming to look for me, but you don't have the right to scold me like a little kid."

He laughed, a mixture of maniacal and impressed–there was that damn smirk again like back at the post office–like he knew better than me.

"Well if you didn't act like a little kid, you wouldn't need to be scolded like one. And trust me, if I wanted to punish you–I would. But not like a kid...oh no. Like a misbehaving bratty woman."

I thought my heart rate couldn't go any faster, but the thought of him punishing me–like a naughty girl...in a way only a man and a woman who could hardly keep their eyes off each other from pure hunger that only escalated, could do. My thighs squeezed together at the thought of what would become of me if I *let* him punish me for my absurd actions. My daydream was interrupted by his continued rampage.

"Because by god, Ginger you could've DIED. Do you understand that??? Are you aware of how dangerous it was? For the love of all the fucking sugar cookies I'm sure you'd prefer to bake in this world, rather than not be here right now; tell me why you went outside tonight."

I slammed my coffee mug down on the table exactly as he had, and faced him like a champion boxer ready to go. Except I was inches below him, have never lifted a hand to another in my life, and I was pretty sure my makeup was smearing at this point, so the overall image had to be hilarious. I wouldn't let that stop me though. I wouldn't let it stop me from giving him a piece of my mind.

"Fine, Colby. I was actually hiding from your overbearing father and that...that...stuck up pretty girl who was wrapped around your arm tonight!! They spoke to me in the hall. They let me know that my presence, my idea for the Christmas festival–which you so valiantly let me fend for all by myself–would not be welcome in their eyes and they'd be watching to see if I mess it all up! I decided after the abysmal night you made for me up on that stage, the fact you apparently don't give a crap about the kiss we shared just a few nights ago, and how I'm hounded by your dad *and* some super model–I needed space to breathe. I was told by a waiter that the lighthouse was open to patrons tonight, so it was the place I thought to go. Happy?!"

Colby took one foot and abruptly pushed away the coffee table–the only thing standing between us–in one, easy sweep. In an instant, he moved closer to me, mere inches, and my fists clenched to hold myself back from running my hands along his chiseled chest. I looked up at him defiantly, unwilling to back down.

"My dad isn't the most savory person, so I'm not surprised. And I swear to you if he does anything to harm your character or reputation here, I'll personally see to it. As for Emma, I'm so sorry. My dad invited her here, she was an ex of mine from over 2 years ago. I was equally as surprised by her appearance. I should've had the guts to tell my father to send her back to California. I was a coward. Something about my dad makes me feel small, weak. Incapable of standing up for myself. I never wanted to hurt you..."

His eyes still blazed with fire even with his words turning over with a sweetness and regret. But I wouldn't bend. Not yet.

"Lastly, as for your question of whether or not I'm happy to hear what happened, my answer is fuck no. My dad was abhorrent, Emma was a mistake, and you—there's no way in this world I'd be happy to know you were made to feel this way or that you could've gotten hurt today."

With this last remark, Colby firmly grabbed my chin and forced me to look at him. Those golden brown eyes that burned with anger, quickly burned with desire. An understanding: he wasn't angry with me, he was *scared* for me. Because Colby Jackson cares.

My lips absent-mindedly parted at the gesture, my hands still balled into fists at my sides, heat seething throughout my body mixed with passion—one that felt like a million suns were exploding and sending shock waves all across my body. He finally let his eyes fall to my lips, licking his own.

"I was wrong to let you think for a single second that there is another girl for me. And if I lost you tonight before I got to explore all of what you bring out in me—all the passion, hope, and zest for life that I've lacked for years, then I would've never recovered from your absence, Cupcake. Your eyes, I fall asleep counting the minutes until they set upon me again. Your lips and the way you bite them when you're thinking too hard, cause my dreams to turn devilish each and every night, wondering when at last I can taste them. Your smile, although rarely happening because of me—I sit and think on how you light up every room you're in like a Christmas tree—one that my mother would've adored."

Tears formed in my eyes, and this time, I couldn't stop them. The whirlwind of emotions this man put me through was enough to make me scream and sigh in relief all at the same time. With his free hand, he wiped a tear away gently–*so gently*. The touch made me crave more.

"You have reawakened a part of me I long thought lost, Ginger. I'm not letting you go, nor letting a single soul hurt you–not even yourself."

Blinking several times to get the tears to hasten their trek, I unclenched my fist and slowly lifted it to lay on his chest.

"I'm sorry, I wasn't meaning to be reckless. I didn't mean to scare you...or make assumptions about you and Emma."

Colby shook his head.

"Don't apologize. It's my fault I didn't say no. If you could forgive me, I promise it won't happen again."

Sighing, I balled his thin shirt into my hand, my chin still caught in his grasp.

"I forgive you."

With that, Colby tightened his grip on my chin again and pulled me closer by the waist with the hand that wiped my tears.

"Good. Then you're going to have to forgive me again, because I still can't stop myself from *punishing* you for nearly tearing my heart from my chest."

The feeling was mutual, but I kept my mouth shut. As soon as the last syllable left his lips, they were on mine, fiercely, hungrily–and I kissed him back just as hard. My arms wrapped tightly around his neck and he pulled me up, lifting me from the ground as I wrapped my legs around his torso, never for a second breaking the kiss. Colby held me tightly as he carried me across the living room to his bedroom, which was filled with dim moonlight from the window. While one hand lowered me down onto his exceptionally soft bed, the other entangled itself in my hair, releasing the pins that held it for the dinner. He finally pulled away from my lips as he relinquished the last pin and threw it to the floor, his breath haggard and his voice in a whisper.

"You don't need that. I love seeing your hair wild, free, exactly like you."

I smiled against his lips, inching my face closer to his again in vain attempt to close the ever-increasing gap.

"My hair's always a mess."

He shook his head and tutted.

"Whoever told you in the past that being messy is a bad thing, never knew how gorgeous you are, just as you are, and that your hair is one of the most unique parts about you. Nor did they know how much I've imagined making it messier, *after making love to you.*"

He brought his lips to barely brush mine, and then teasingly kissed my chin, leaving lingering kisses along my jawline and neck. I writhed beneath him, his hand still holding my hair, the other beginning to roam up my thigh, my already lifting green evening dress rising further with it. My breath stifled, which only egged him on while he nipped at my collarbone. I gasped out a response. The moment was sexy, pure fire raging between us, and yet I couldn't help but continue the banter that made me fall harder for him, **the banter, only we could do**. After all, tension and anger are quite similar to lust and love–right?

"Mmm...speaking of messy...I was expecting your room to be less tidy. And considering the state of your poor couch, I'm amazed at the quality of your sheets."

Colby nipped me again harder, his mouth having already lowered to the top of my bedazzled decolletage, right above my heart. I moaned in response, my hands grabbing at his shirt and lifting it slightly, allowing my fingers to graze the skin around his waist. He sucked in air, and I smiled with triumph. He spoke again between nips along my chest.

"I may not be the most acquainted with house decor, but I'm not a savage. Soft sheets make for better sleep...or better..."

His voice trailed off, suggestions oozing from every word. But I didn't want to keep hearing suggestions. I wanted results. I would *not* let this man infuriate me any longer today. I ran my hand through his hair and tugged, lifting his mouth off me. He looked at me with a raised eyebrow before I pushed him off, rolling him onto his back, and climbing on top, straddling him. The way his eyes opened and quickly honed in on the way my hips rested on his most sensitive area. He let out a small moan which made me hunger for more.

Leaning down, I grabbed his curled locks and made him look at me while I whispered.

"Oh shush."

And I shut him up with the most passionate kiss I could.

15

Hark the Festival

Colby

After our night together, I forced Ginger to show me her magic for over 2 hours the following morning during breakfast, many of which included pouring out coffee into the cups without her hands or picking up the salt shaker for our omelets she made with her magic. Her hair was in an updo for the first time since I've met her, and although she was slightly embarrassed for her pointed ears, I couldn't stop thinking how she could possibly get more adorable. She would, however, swat me away each time I came behind her to touch them.

Safe to say, I annoyed her until she was scolding me—but I was absolutely fascinated. I was not one to believe in magic or other creatures, but how could I look past the impossibly sexy girl standing in my kitchen, untying her destroyed cocktail dress from behind with nothing more than a flick of the wrist.

However, that trick didn't get my praise. I kissed her with force, letting her know *that* part would always be my job—magic be damned.

Afterwards when we were both hustling out the cottage door, shamelessly fixing each other's clothes, we walked together into the square as she told me that Izabelle was an Elf, too.

"That punk princess is an Elf? How did that happen?"

I found Izabelle being a Christmas Elf more shocking than Ginger–black hair with red highlights and a scowl that could cut through ice, didn't seem to match the typical holiday vibes in any of the Christmas stories I read as a kid. The pure contradiction was enough to elicit multiple laughing fits from me, Ginger swatting me to behave, and reminding me not to let Izabelle know that I knew what she was. The secrecy wasn't all that apparent to me, but I knew it was risky business, and I wouldn't do anything to put either of them in more trouble. I sealed the promise with a hastened kiss before sauntering to city hall, turning back for one last look at her while she entered the café, those luscious curls bouncing with every step.

Since then, we've spent every spare second together over the last few days planning the events for the new and improved Christmas festival that's starting today. Between her running back and forth at the café once she informed Izabelle she was safe and got a reprimanding even worse than mine, and me running every ridiculously made-up errand my father could throw at me to distract me from assisting with the festival organization, our moments together beyond that were typically brief, but very ***hot***.

Luckily, Zeus and her cat Gimli got along, and Gimli already knew how to get in my place through a window whenever he pleased while Ginger was there. Zeus seemed to love the company.

The rejuvenation I was feeling while planning the events was something I haven't felt in years. With each vendor we booked, each decoration we put up in the town square, and each time I accidentally brushed Ginger's hand or *un-accidentally* pulled her into an alleyway to kiss those perfect lips again, I was feeling lighter–whole again. And I was finding my mom everywhere, and it was the best feeling in the world to feel her close again.

Even though we hadn't spoken again about Ginger's predicament, I felt a nervousness from her I didn't recognize. Since the night of the dinner, she didn't want to discuss the North Pole or what her consequences might be for revealing herself to a human. She continued to be peppy and was putting all her energy into the festival, but I know something is wrong. Whenever she hears a noise behind us while hanging wreaths on the lampposts, she jumps a foot in the air and can't stop looking around corners. She's afraid, and part of me is saddened she won't tell me why. I mean, it's not like Santa sends out assassins, right?

Ginger has assured me it isn't my burden, but with each passing day, with every kiss and every touch, I am yearning more and more to be part of that burden. I haven't loved a woman since Emma, which is still keeping her hip attached to my dad's. And thinking now on the relationship since she's come back; I question whether there had been real love there at all.

It was different with Ginger, she didn't want me to take on anything because she didn't need me to; while Emma thought I should do everything for her out of principle because she believed she was a trophy.

Ginger did her best to make me know I didn't need to do anything for her. But fuck, I *want* to. For the first time since my mom died, I really want to take care of somebody. I *want* Ginger to lay her burdens on the bed we've shared and let me help put them in order. I *want* her to confide in me so I can comfort and support her. And dammit, I *want* to be her man in every sense, because she is healing me with her kindness. Curing me with her spirit. And absolutely driving me crazy with the way I want to be with her every moment. She is showing me I don't have to hide from my grief, but that I can live with it and still find joy.

I can find my mom everywhere and it does not have to break me down; but lift me up.

We still haven't told anybody about our secret relationship, as she asked to keep it quiet for the sake of her mission. When I asked how I could help raise the Christmas Spirit or whatever she needed, she kissed me softly and said, "You already are helping." She showed me this strange cellphone with red and green lights indicating the spirit levels, which have promptly risen 25% since we announced the Christmas festival revival. She was anticipating it getting higher as the week progressed, with today being the first event of the festival and ending with a grand ball Christmas Eve night.

I was able to convince my dad to allow us to convert the town hall auditorium into our ball space. With its domed loft space, large windows, ample room for both dancing and catering, and an ornate crystal chandelier that dated back to the late 1800s, it was the best option to fit the entire town. Once removing the seating for usual

council and city meetings, I couldn't picture a better place. Suffice it
to say, Ginger was thrilled!

I was on my way to the square to meet her and begin the first
event: the Christmas tree farm and market. We'd been able to contact
a local tree farm to set up in the square with trees for families to
purchase, and some vendors with food and games set up, including
sack racing. Izabelle would set a booth for coffee and hot chocolate
while I assisted Ginger with keeping everyone happy and the event
on track. The hype around the start of the festival was buzzing all
around town, and I couldn't wait to get there.

After dropping off the final letters my aunt brought to my
dad's empty office, she kissed my cheek and told me how proud she
was–for bringing back the festival, and for rekindling things with
Ginger. She added that my mother would be over the moon, in more
ways than one. I couldn't help but hold back a tear when she said it.
After grabbing Zeus, who was waiting in the front lobby, I rushed to
the square; the market was about to kick off!

Zeus and I made our way towards the heart of the town, the
snow in splotches on the ground from a few days hiatus from a recent
flurry, but still made for a beautiful wintry sight when I started to
see the bundled fir trees lined up by height and width; the scent
from them was calming and inviting. Zeus was happily panting as
we approached Ginger, who was wearing an Elf costume.

Except, now that I think of it, perhaps I should be calling it an
Elf *uniform*.

With a bright green, velvet dress with long sleeves ending in
white fluff around the cuffs and a skirt flaring out at the waist, but

ending just below the butt, with more fluff trimming the ends. If it wasn't for the ridiculous candy cane colored leggings beneath, the dress wouldn't leave much to the imagination. The pièce de résistance of the entire ensemble was the matching velvet hat that sat on her head like Santa's, barely staying atop her wild, red curls, which she had as neatly as she could, in a long braid that draped over one shoulder. A few of her signature curls still fell down in ringlets that framed her face, and the puff ball drooped down in the same fashion.

Overall, she was absolutely adorable and looked more like herself than I'd ever seen her. With Ginger already being so quirky, this fit naturally. She was made to be an Elf. With her personality being bubbly with a kick, and how cheery and kind she was to everyone around her, it was the most fitting thing in the world to see her this way. I didn't know what was cuter, the way she fussed about trying to put finishing touches on the welcome sign she was sitting up, or the way she fussed with trying to sling that damn puff ball out of her face.

*Oh how I'd love to grab her from behind, spin her around, and kiss those perfect, cherry-red lips. Her cheeks turning rosy, but not from the cold, but from the **heat**.*

I considered doing just that when Zeus bounded towards Ginger and panted at her feet happily. She stopped what she was doing and kneeled down to hug him and kiss his nose–like she'd always been a part of his life. The gesture made my heart full; Zeus was a big part of my life and had been since my mother's passing. He was the friend who got me through the hardest part of it, that companion I so desperately needed when talking to other humans became a chore rather than a relief. I'm not sure where I'd be if I didn't have Zeus, because he truly was the reason I could get out of bed some days; and he never judged, never sent obnoxious "I'm sorry" gifts right when she passed when the people wouldn't even talk to me weeks later, nor would he tell me to "just get over it and get out there again." He was loyal, faithful, and cheered me up more than anything else did in those early days. He's been that rock I clung to and kept my head above water when the tides of grief tried to pull me under.

To see his connection with Ginger so genuinely match my own, I could swear I saw love hearts in the air like an old cartoon when I look at the two of them together. As I approached, Gimli was hanging out in the cat tower, Ginger typically used in the café by the front window. I went to scratch the broody little furball, and he meowed in response, a pleasant enough greeting. In reality, the personalities of our pets should match the other person more: Zeus and Ginger had so much energy and brightness, while Gimli and I would rather not be bothered by most.

What a funny thing, hm?

Gimli meowed again a bit louder, and Ginger piped up in agitation.

"Gimli, you do not need to be so rude to Colby. He doesn't know you as well as I do; how would he know that where he scratched you wasn't where you prefer?"

I looked down at the fussy cat and put my hands up jokingly in defense.

"I thought cats liked their chins scratched! My bad, your *highness*."

Gimli made another indiscernible sound, which Ginger huffed at.

"Oh yes, Gimli. You are definitely not like most cats. Give him a break, he'll figure it out. And don't get used to being called your highness, you pompous little feline."

I laughed for more reasons than one; the fact that I was getting scolded by a cat and the fact Ginger knew it. She'd told me by now she could speak to animals, and even though she began doing it far more openly with me around to not only Gimli, but Zeus as well, it was still quite the adjustment to get used the the fact Zeus let me know yesterday he preferred his food heated up for a few seconds rather than cold. I asked Ginger if I was destined to be bossed by my dog now that he had a messenger, and her response was, "Only if you keep me around!" She proceeded to wink at me, and Zeus barked for his dinner. All in all, it's been an exciting and revealing week together. And Zeus is now more pampered than I think he's ever been.

I rounded behind Ginger as she finished placing the welcome sign she'd painted with gorgeous swirling calligraphy, and stood closely beside her, my voice a whisper.

"Do you think I will ever get Gimli's seal of approval?"

She turned those green eyes on me, raising an eyebrow.

"You think he'd let you stick around so much if you hadn't already?"

She bit her lip the way I've noticed she tends to when she's deep in thought or nervous. We've been intimate on more than one occasion already, but our relationship wasn't public nor did we truly understand what *it* was. Whenever she got to thinking of us as something more, she bit her lip in anxiety, and even though I felt just as torn up about how this might play out after Christmas, I also couldn't help but melt when she did it. Her worried eyes lingered on mine for a moment, and I wondered if I could steal a kiss and help make those worries go away, even for a second. I steadied myself though; I wouldn't do anything to jeopardize her already difficult situation with Headquarters, as she called it.

Instead, I turned to look around to see Izabelle across the way, setting up the coffee station under her tent. Another table was set up beside her booth with undecorated sugar cookies and icing supplies–the cookie decorating station was Ginger's personal touch. The local burger joint owners were inside their trailer, the smell wafted through the air towards me. In the middle of the square were dozens upon dozens of beautiful fir trees lined up for picking. The light posts were adorned with wreaths and bows, and we'd set up some Christmas backdrops for photos. Our resident Santa Claus, Mr. Jenkins–the same cheerful old man who'd played Santa at our festival longer than I can remember–sat proudly in front of one of the backdrops, looking as happy as ever in his renewed role. Off towards Mr. Jenkins' right, was where the sack racing was set up with a start and finish line prominently placed.

The sight of the square lit a fire inside me, a magical feeling seemed to settle over the area, and I wondered if Ginger had something to do with enhancing the beauty of it all, or if she studied holiday decoration while in training at the North Pole. A crowd was beginning to form along the edges of the event, and the excitement and bustle was electrifying. Ginger grabbed a large wooden box, standing on it as Izabelle came over to hand her a microphone which was connected to a speaker that would play music shortly once the event began.

Clearing her throat, the crowd huddled closer, looking around in awe at the decorations and activities; there was no denying it was a sight to behold. For the first time in 5 years the square was decorated for the holidays, and it was all due to that little Elf needing to stand on a box to see above the crowd. Ginger patted the microphone to check it before speaking.

"Hello everybody! Welcome to the first annual Everly's Yuletide Festival! In honor of Colby's mother, Everly Jackson, we are here today, and all week, to celebrate her life and love of all things Christmas. From what Colby has told me, Everly would've been a lady I could connect with. She was lively, personable, and kind beyond reproach. She implemented the first Christmas festival years ago, and it is our honor to rejuvenate it in her name. There will be events and markets for the next couple of weeks, and we're ending with a grand ball on Christmas Eve. All proceeds from ticket sales for the ball will be given to a foundation for Dementia—so please, order your tickets and enjoy the fun and togetherness!"

Ginger paused and looked at me, a tear having formed in my eyes at her declaration, but I brushed my coat off and looked back at the crowd, whose energy only heightened at Ginger's words.

"And now...please, come enjoy the food, drinks, and games we have! Oh, and don't forget Santa is on site today; go give him a great big hug and let him know all your Christmas wishes!"

A loud, vigorous applause from the people ended shortly after, and everyone began checking out what goodies were in store. Many immediately went to grab hot cocoa or coffee from Izabelle, several kids already waiting in line for Santa. Mr. Jenkins smiled so big, I swore he looked to be the real Santa if I ever saw one. Even Ginger praised him, saying he was as close to the real deal as she's ever seen.

Ginger stepped off the platform and shrugged her shoulders.

"Welp, we did it! We successfully set up the first event!"

"We did indeed, and it's all thanks to you. Everyone looks so happy, I bet your Spiritometer is going off the charts right now."

She blushed.

"I hope so! It's unfortunately at Izabelle's station; these tights don't leave room for much!"

I let my eyes roam down her legs and back up. Even in the ridiculous get-up, she was stunning–and *delicious*. It didn't matter how much we needed to behave ourselves, my hands itched at my sides to run along those legs and hold her tight. I licked my lips and met her eyes again.

"Oh no, they don't. Don't change."

Ginger shushed me promptly.

"Shhh...someone could hear us, Colby."

"Let them. Come on. They wouldn't think it's odd, we've been spending the whole last week together planning this; they'd just think it's some Christmas miracle you were able to finally thaw this frozen heart. Proximity does often lead to more...It wouldn't be so weird, would it?"

She bit her lip again...that anxiety was back.

"Colby...I want to. But you know I could get into trouble. Elves and humans aren't supposed to be together. I broke so many rules and...and the consequences are too great. We have to lay low until the holidays are over. Please, give me a little more time to figure this out."

Even though it felt like my chest was briefly stomped on, I let out a large sigh and kicked the snow at my feet.

"Of course. I don't want to do anything to make it worse. We will take it day by day, okay?"

Geez, what did this girl do to me? Old me would be confused. Before, I tended to want to keep relationships from going public, not practically begging at a tiny woman's feet to *actually* do it.

She finally smiled at me, but her smile quickly faded when her eyes darted behind me. A small cough signaled what I'd almost forgotten about.

Theo Jackson had arrived.

16

Alleyways Best Kept Secret

O ver Colby's shoulder, I met the eyes I dreaded to see the most: Mr. Jackson's blue irises glancing dismissively at me. As Colby turned, I finally saw the Wicked Witch of Everly Cove right alongside him–Emma. Both glared at me as if I was the absolute bane of their existence. If only they knew how mutual the feeling was.

Colby stood taller, in a defensive stance, one I hadn't seen before. He looked over both of them and didn't say a word. When Mr. Jackson finally spoke, the cheerful noise of the patrons enjoying the market was brought to inaudible levels, my heartbeat was outweighing everything else.

"Good morning, Colby. *Ginger*. What an interesting choice for a first event. Creating your own makeshift tree farm, not a bad touch."

Colby's voice was grave, and he responded with so much disdain, it made me temporarily forget he was talking to his own dad.

"Thanks, Dad. Mom would've loved all of it."

Emma choked back a laugh. She wore a ridiculous fur hat that stood straight up like a bucket, and her black coat went all the way down nearly to her ankles, barely revealing a pair of insanely expensive white heeled boots which matched the hat. At the exact moment she laughed, Zeus, who'd been sitting beside Colby, bounded toward her in excitement and tried to jump on her. Emma screamed, backing away.

"No, no..no Zeus! These are my new shoes! Colby, would you mind controlling him??"

Colby rolled his eyes and called Zeus back, patting his head reassuringly when he sat beside him again. His face had grown sad and it made me want to just take a flick of my wrist and send her sailing down an icy path as far away from me as possible; but I couldn't do my magic in public–especially not for a reason like that.

Okay, so calling her a witch doesn't quite cut it, what about our own personal Cruella?

Once settled, Emma's attention turned to me. She eyed my outfit up and down, and the uniform I usually felt so confident in was now making me feel I'd rather cover myself in one of the burlap sacks from the race. She propped an arm up, looking like she was inspecting my outfit like a fashion designer who saw the most disgusting thing of their career.

"Oh, you poor thing. Whoever volunteered you to wear that must be playing a prank on you. If your height didn't make you look like a little girl, this outfit surely does! I wouldn't be caught dead in such a thing."

I had zero words. My usual fiery temper wasn't coming to defend me. I just continued to stand there like a fool, in green, velvet pointed shoes and striped stockings.

Colby's fist clenched at his side, his eyes shooting daggers at Emma even worse than the ones he tossed his dad.

"You wouldn't be caught dead in that outfit only because you have the personality of a viper; children would run scared of you, while children, not to mention everybody, *adore* Ginger. People flock to her because it doesn't matter if she's wearing a costume; she is always who she is: one of the most incredible women I've ever met. So you're right, if you wore something like this, I'd know it wasn't really you."

My cheeks turned a bright red, my mouth opened to speak, but no words came out.

*Colby is literally defending me–in such a **personal** way.*

Don't get me wrong, it was one of the nicest compliments I've ever heard in my life. But it also puts a target on my back–because it made it sound like Colby cared for me more than a colleague or even a friend...but like a *lover*. And with my current predicament, I couldn't risk our relationship being discovered. Not when I needed to raise Christmas Spirit levels to make sure Santa could go on his trek in the first place, and not to mention, I needed to save Colby. I couldn't let his memory be erased.

This was the exact reason we needed to tread carefully, but his defense of me could raise eyebrows, and Emma was now looking at me a little differently than before. I could only hope it didn't raise enough suspicion just yet. When she at last looked away, like I was more of a nuisance rather than a romantic rival, I was able to let go of the breath I'd been holding. Mr. Jackson raised an eyebrow at his son, looking surprised at his retaliation. He adjusted his scarf, one similar to what I'd seen Colby wear before, the navy and maroon knitted one. I wondered if it was one they each got from his mother. After tugging it a bit higher around his chin, he smiled at the both of us and held an arm out for Emma to take.

"Yes, the townspeople have certainly grown attached to our newest addition. I do hope there won't be any disappointments during this highly anticipated festival. Your mother would be sad if her legacy was tainted."

I felt tears threaten my eyes, but I only stared at Mr. Jackson and held them back. I wouldn't dare let him make me cry again. Colby's hand flexed like he wanted nothing more than to hold my hand, but he didn't make the final move to do so.

"Mom would've loved this. All of it. And the best part would be the fact her son was involved and the happiest he's been in years. Not to mention how happy the rest of the town is. She wouldn't be disappointed in anything. She'd be *thrilled*."

Mr. Jackson swallowed, unable to come up with a retort, and linked arms with Emma as they walked over to inspect the remainder of the event. I knew my heart was thudding wildly, and my anxiety about the prospects of this Christmas and the stakes being so high, were weighing on me like I was stuck beneath Santa's sleigh.

As soon as they were out of sight, Colby turned to me, his fists still clenched. He spoke with a severe guilt behind his voice.

"I'm so sorry for what they said. I knew they'd always been hard on me, but to hear how cruel they both were to you...it is ripping my insides to shreds. You don't deserve any of it, and my dad knows it."

I watched as Colby looked after where his father and Emma disappeared, and I didn't know quite what to say. He wasn't wrong, I didn't deserve it. But he had a long, drawn-out, and difficult history with both of them. It was no wonder when a new person came in and flipped the town upside down, and flipped *Colby* upside down too–there would be some backlash. He'd told me how it ended with Emma after our first night together, and I've heard bits and pieces of the discontent he's had with his dad since his mother passed away, but it didn't prepare me for the onslaught I was encountering with each passing day in Everly Cove. My idea that the festival would be good for everyone, wasn't at all the case. Each day I was here, the clock was ticking faster and faster, and I was nowhere near close enough to getting Spirit back to 100% here, which the Pole desperately needed.

Without the Spirit levels returning to its once former glory, there wouldn't be enough energy to lift the sleigh off the ground Christmas Eve.

Children all over the world would wake up to find there was truly no Santa Claus, and the moment that happened, Christmas as we know it would be doomed. The finite levels of Spirit we had left would be depleted the moment millions of children came to no longer believe in Santa. It would be over, and all of it would be entirely *my* fault.

Now to top off the pressure, I was being looked at as some sort of villain by the town mayor and the petty ex-girlfriend of the man I shouldn't be sleeping with. Or falling for...

I not only broke every Elven rule you can possibly break when it comes to human interactions, I also put the first man I have ever come close to loving, at risk.

*Ah! Ginger! You don't love, Colby. Get it together, okay. You **can't** love him.*

I wasn't sure how I was going to make it through the rest of this mission. But as sure as jingle bells ring, I cannot let myself fall in love with someone who won't remember I exist after Christmas.

"Hurt people, hurt people. Your dad is just using it as a defense mechanism for his wife. He worries this won't live up to what she deserves, and your mother deserves the best. He's only protecting her. And Emma...well Emma is a scorned ex. She wants you back, otherwise she wouldn't have come when your father sent the invitation. I'll be okay, but thank you for what you said."

Colby looked as if he wanted to say more, but I whirled around and waited for Gimli who meowed a faint response as I looked at him, letting me know he would continue meandering the market with Zeus. I nodded at him, avoiding further eye contact with Colby, and made my way as fast as possible towards Izabelle and hopefully, a relief from the sitcom my life has seemingly become.

It wasn't necessarily Colby's fault; he in fact defended me. Quite romantically, if I think back on it...but in the end, although Spirit has increased since my arrival, it wasn't close enough to fixing our problem. And Colby was quickly becoming someone I cared for, but that didn't mean in the end it would be a 'Happily Elf Ever After' for me. In fact, it was bound to end in heartbreak, and a long list of memories left forgotten.

At least for one of us.

As for me, I would go on for the rest of my long life and forever be burned with the taste of his lips on mine, or the way his strong hands curl along my spine when we make love, to tease me in a way that has me begging for more. I would never be able to forget him, but in two seconds with the flash of the Pole's coveted memory eraser: Colby Jackson would never remember we met, or kissed, or how my heart palpitates by how he says my name when he wakes up sleepy, rolling over in bed searching for me–like I was missed even while dreaming.

As if all of that hurt weren't enough, if I didn't succeed in my task in Everly Cove, Christmas would cease to exist. And it would all be my fault. So what was I getting hung up on some guy for when the joy and happiness of the world was at stake? Could I really be this selfish as to not only have a relationship with a human, which is strictly forbidden, hide it from my people who have put their trust in me, and then hide the consequences of what will happen when they find out from Colby, to top it all off?

This has got to go down as the worst moment in Elf history: Ginger Tinsel finds a way to break a man's heart, let her entire people down, and ruin Christmas forever–in one single month.

I rushed my way towards Izabelle who'd just handed a wily toddler a cup of hot cocoa, which was then tested for risk of possible burns by the overprotective mother, to which Izabelle smiled politely.

"For children's cocoa, I always lower the heat index, but let me know if I can make it even cooler for you."

If I wasn't so upset about the interaction with Mr. Jackson and Emma's scathing review on my outfit of choice today, I would've reminded Izabelle that although she has worked graciously on her tone while in Everly Cove, her sarcasm still leaked out all over the place. It wasn't her fault though. She'd made it this far in the ranks in the North Pole because of her hard attitude and even harder work ethic; she is far out-ranking me in the department. She only took this position as a favor to my sister; she didn't *have* to be here. Customer service was not her forte, having always been reprimanded for her lack of social etiquette, even back at the Pole. But she was a heck of a friend and confidant since arriving here, and her special ability to ease people around her didn't hurt. And despite my issues with my sister, if Clara trusted her, then so did I. The only issue is Izabelle still doesn't know about my relationship with Colby.

After the lady gave a vicious sneer, that quickly turned to complacency–Izabelle's magic aiding the interaction–her shoulders dropped in the act of "playing nice" like we'd been practicing, and her usual chilly exterior was back in place by the time I shuffled my way behind the booth we set up for the event, and stood next to the space heater she'd plugged in. The cold didn't affect me much, but it seemed to always affect Izabelle, which was hilarious considering we live in the coldest place on Earth. I teased her about the affliction once, and she said if I ever mentioned it to anyone, she'd make sure

I wouldn't be baking gingerbread cookies ever again; I booped her nose and said I would never tell a soul. This too, she made me swear to never mention. But I think she secretly likes me enough to let it slide.

Izabelle watched silently as I folded my arms over my chest and looked around the square. People were scurrying around happily, and it honestly made my heart soar to see. But in the same instant, my heart skittered at an alarming rate, and I wondered if Izabelle would need to perform CPR when I passed out from anxiety. When I didn't bring myself to speak, Izabelle turned to me, chewing on a stopper for the coffee cups, looking like someone out of one of those old mobster movies where the badass was always chewing on a cigar or toothpick. She spoke through the stopper still hanging out of the side of her mouth.

"Wanna talk about it?"

I continued to look around anxiously, half-anticipating to see Emma dart out like a spooky clown on Halloween and give me a jump scare. I knew I was being paranoid, but I couldn't deal with the horror of another berating for the time being. Also, I'd like to avoid the guilt of building an event in the honor of a woman I hadn't known and continue to get the death glare from the father of the guy I was in bed with each night. *No, thank you.* However, Izabelle was not one to be ignored, so I hugged myself a little tighter.

"Well, I think it's well known that Mr. Jackson does not like me at all. He thinks I'm tarnishing his wife's reputation, and to be honest, maybe I am."

Izabelle raised an eyebrow at me.

"What are you talking about? From everything you've relayed and what Colby has said about his mom, she would've loved every second of this."

I reached for a to-go cup and poured a steaming cup of cocoa for myself; not because I necessarily needed it, but I needed to distract myself, even just for a moment.

"Yeah, Colby said the same thing when he defended me openly in front of his dad...and Emma."

The entire time Colby and I have been getting together after event planning, Izabelle assumed I'd been going home for much-needed rest. Little did she know, rest was far and few between with Colby–but back-to-back, toe-curling releases? Well, those were in abundance. As were the talks. The conversation about our true dreams in life: me baking and him going to culinary school. It was the greatest part of our relationship. He too, was dealt with an overbearing dad who wished he'd follow in the family footsteps, while I dealt with a sister who couldn't find the line between her life and mine; not to mention how Elves weren't allowed to change stations or career paths.

We found we had a lot in common, a lot of goals and promises we'd made to ourselves we were afraid we would never realize. It was one of the reasons I was falling for Colby the most. How his eyes lit up describing a new dish he created for dinner once, or how he expressed his greatest dread walking into his father's office at town hall each day to hear the newest scheme he'd concocted on how to convince his only son to take up arms and join politics. Lying in each other's arms after our intimate time and being completely ourselves, no masks or pretending–in total peace. It was truly something I've never experienced before.

But if I told Izabelle this, then it could put her job in jeopardy as well. That was something I couldn't drag her into; she didn't come here to suffer from my mistakes.

"He defended you openly? That's something, considering he pretty much ignored your existence at the dinner party. Which, by the way, I'm still not over how he acted towards you. And the ex? Oof! Perhaps they deserve each other after all."

Izabelle didn't know Colby the way I did, but hearing her disparaging comments about him made my heart twist in a knot. Unfortunately, Izabelle hadn't seen Colby since the night of the dinner party and had a lot to say about his behavior, which she often chided me about keeping clear of him unless absolutely necessary.

Guess I ignored that memo...

I bit my lip and shook my head in agreement.

"Yeah, it surprised me, too."

*Well, at least **that** wasn't a lie.*

Izabelle eyed me over. She knew I was keeping something, but she was polite enough not to push like my sister would've. It's one of the many reasons I adored Izabelle so much. We may be exact opposites, but she was truly a friend I could count on. I took my attention to the swarming crowds of the town square, finding it hard not to smile at the joy that filled the space. This may very well be the happiest the town has been in years, feeling like the dark cloud that was hiding this adorable town was finally lifting. Children laughed and adults were happily sipping cocoa, warming mittens, families picking out the perfect tree...it was all the magic of Christmas that it should be.

I continued to sip my cocoa trying to come up with something to say, but words were totally escaping me–and my anxiety was peaking past a point I wasn't sure I'd be able to handle much longer. Perhaps if I took a look at my Spiritometer, the increased Christmas Spirit might cheer me up and not make me feel like an absolute failure.

"Uh...I'm going to go check on the progress of our...levels. Are you good here?"

Izabelle smiled, and I swear I thought I'd fall over in shock.

"I'm fantastic actually; this is the most fun I've had in forever. I really enjoy interacting with the kids."

Seeing Izabelle light up from working on this mission and the growth I've witnessed in her, it really was remarkable. She might look a bit tough on the outside, but on the inside, she was a gooey marshmallow. I smiled back at her and grabbed the little device from under the counter. With a wave, I slipped out of the booth, heading down a vacant street near the ice sculpture area. Only a couple of older gentlemen were there, too engrossed in what they were doing to notice me slip past. I ducked behind the wall and pulled out the Spiritometer.

Location: Everly Cove, Maine
Time: 1:58 pm
Christmas Spirit Scale: 67%

"Thank all that is merry and bright!! We are so close!"

It was such a relief to see the status of Spirit here in Everly Cove, with only a few days left of events before Christmas. It was hard to believe where the levels started when I arrived here. But seeing the amount of happiness and participation from the townspeople, it was a wonder! Maybe I was always meant to be the one to make it happen–to save Christmas. If I didn't run into Colby that first day at the post office, perhaps none of this would be possible. I would've never known the town was suffering from a suffocating grief that wouldn't let go, or that the culprit was the mayor himself having stopped the Christmas festival to begin with–I would've never met Colby and seen the bright star he actually was in this town. The level was sitting squarely at 64%, and I couldn't be happier! We still had some work to do, but with another week's worth of activities and the ball? We were an Elf's shoo-in to pull this off!

All of a sudden, I heard a throat clear nearby, and nearly jumped out of my skin, until Colby peered around the corner of the street building. Putting a finger over his lips to shush me.

"For Frosty's sake, Colby! You nearly gave me a heart attack!"

He shrugged his shoulders and ticked his tongue, wagging a finger at me.

"Well, maybe you shouldn't be sneaking down alleyways when there's a whole festival in need of your attention, Miss."

I rolled my eyes, tucking my Spiritometer back inside the waistband of my skirt until I could drop it off with Izabelle again. Lifting my eyes back to Colby's as he made his way dangerously close to me, I folded my arms over my chest to try and hide the escalating heartbeat Colby always incited when he was close.

"You sir, shouldn't be following women down said alleyways. People might think you're up to something you shouldn't be."

Colby's eyebrow curled up in a mischievous way as he looked me up and down, not in the way Emma had done earlier, where it was out of spite, but in a way that made my toes curl in my pointed Elf booties.

"What if I am? What if I haven't been able to get my mind off wanting to kiss you...*all...day...****long.***"

His words came out breathy, slow, *sensual*. The air I sucked in caught in my throat as he quickly closed the gap between us, his hands splaying out on the brick wall above my head, enclosing me beneath his body. My chest heaved, and his golden brown eyes looked at me with pure, unadulterated desire. Leaning down, he whispered, his lips just barely touching my own.

"What if not being able to touch you all day is killing me? What if pretending like you don't capture every thought or how you dictate my every fucking action in the day...feels wrong. What if..."

He paused, his heavy breathing now matching my own. One hand fell down at my waist, the other still holding its place; making sure I'm pinned to the wall beneath him. The free hand gripped my waist hard, and slowly slid upwards, making the fuzzy hem of my skirt rise higher, until he forcefully pulled the fabric of my skirt and brought our bodies smashing together. My hands itching to touch him, unable to hold back any longer, grabbing the front of his jacket in an attempt to pull him as close as possible to me. He smirked that annoyingly sexy smirk that lets me know he's up to no good. The hand on the wall suddenly grabbed both of my wrists in one hand, and pulled them high above my head, restraining them in a firm grasp–*and I was now totally at his mercy.*

I twisted beneath him, and the hand gripping my skirt grabbed my waist forcefully, holding me in place. His eyes are swimming with all the memories of our nightly routine recently, and I could practically beg him to take me back home right here, right now in the middle of this festival hung in the air between us. At last, he bit my bottom lip ravenously and made me moan, heat curling in my core.

"What if I want everybody to know *you're mine*, Ginger Tinsel?"

Before I can respond, his mouth is on me with a fiery desperation I hadn't encountered with him before. The kiss was eager and hungry. His tongue swept in my mouth hungrily and I matched the energy, his body pressing against mine, his hand running along my ribs, up to tickle the side of my breast teasingly. The heat that consumed my body felt like I might burn through this outfit.

When I think I can't contain the tension any longer, Colby brings the kiss down a notch, but still not lacking any intensity. It turns from fiery, to gentle–slowly releasing my hands and carefully taking a hold of my chin to look into his eyes as the kiss finally breaks, my body still squirming for more.

"Just a taste to get through. Since we will both be busy the next couple of days, and I know Izabelle needs some help back at the café to prepare for the ball, I have a surprise for you the evening before Christmas Eve. My place, 8'o clock, sharp. Until then..."

Colby kisses me again, and I savor every single second of his mouth hot against me. With my newly freed hands, I reach up to wrap my arms around his neck, the actions forcing me on my tiptoes, which he assists by lifting me up to hold me closer. I run my hand through his tight curls and luxuriate in the softness I have come to know so well. 3 nights away from him was a necessity, but not something I thought I'd hate so much.

Izabelle and I were fully catering the Christmas ball, and it was far more complicated than the one cake I did for the dinner party. Izabelle didn't say it, but she was running ragged from the extra buzz around the time, which included extra customers at the café. It was amazing to know so many people from out of town were coming in for the festival, making the town revitalize to its former glory—but that meant all hands on deck, and Izabelle was no cook. It was my time to come back to help with that, and leave the remainder of the ball decorations and ticket sales to Colby.

But that meant I needed to stay late baking, and would need to help Izabelle more rather than spend the nights in Colby's arms. It was only a few days. How could this possibly feel like absolute agony? When we'd made the plan at the start of recreating the festival, it was an easy decision to make the most of the last few days working with Izabelle on the menu.

Now, an ache in my chest pulsed at the realization I wouldn't see Colby much until then. To know I won't fall asleep in his strong, comforting embrace. To know I won't get to see the adorable bed head I've come to find so endearing. To know I won't touch him, *be* touched *by* him in the way that makes my skin pebble with goosebumps, only he knows how to cause–this would be harder than I thought.

The man who rudely upended my Elfish life when I walked into town, the man who made me roll my eyes and do my best to be out of his company at the opening, the man who nearly broke my heart when I saw Emma latched to his arm at the party, was now the man who I was falling harder for than anyone else before.

How could I have gotten myself into such a mess for a man whom I'm quite literally breaking all the rules for? I'm risking my livelihood, my traditions, and the honor of the long line of proud Tinsels. The risk of Christmas falling apart at my feet was still prominent. And yet, when he kisses me like this, all I crave is a lifetime of it.

Colby pulled away, but I continued to clutch his jacket tightly. Slightly out of breath, I met his amber gaze.

"A surprise you say?"

Colby pecked my nose and smiled.

"Mhm. One I think you'll love."

I leaned up and stole one last kiss, Colby chuckling and moving the stubborn red curl that persistently gave me hell, out of my face, tucking neatly under my hat, which he sweetly adjusted, before saluting at me as he walked back towards the market.

"You get that Christmas Spirit up now, got it? Work that adorable Elf charm; and until we can be public, just know I'll be nearby, daydreaming of your body beneath me every chance I get over the next several days."

When he was around the corner, I felt happy enough to squeal. Spirit levels were rising fast. The festival was hitting off perfectly. And perhaps, if my mission succeeds, I could find a way to convince the Elf council to let me stay in a relationship with Colby. Not that we'd defined the relationship...but something was defrosting that ol' grumpy Snowman's heart, and there was no way I was going to let him go that easily. I'm Ginger, after all. I can find my way out of anything if I'm determined enough. I'll find a way to save Christmas and be with the man who made me melt like a freshly fallen snowflake.

A gasp alerted me to someone at the other end of the alley.

"Oh. My. God. You're *with* Colby??"

Emma's raspy tone made my heart drop into my stomach fast.

Looks like our secret isn't so secret anymore.

17

Throwing Shade (& Snow)

Ginger

Emma stomps her perfectly white-heeled boots my way to stand right in front of me like she's going to fight. Our height difference gives her the advantage, but I'm speedy if I need to be. And her comments over the last few weeks have really turned me sour. If she's come to fight, this Elf knows how to be scrappy; who says good Elves can't get a little bad?

I eye her questioningly, but my nerves are jumping about in my body like a springboard. My magic doesn't like confrontation, and I can feel the energy begin to sizzle in my fingertips. What first came out like anger, quickly turned to panic.

Had she heard what Colby said about me being an Elf? How long was she standing there watching us?

"Kind of weird you'd be standing there in an alleyway like that just watching us, don't you think, Emma?"

She screwed up her nose at me.

"I came looking for Colby. I couldn't find him anywhere; his father needed him. Then I found the two of you and couldn't hold back my shock."

I knew she was lying, she must've been looking for Colby for herself. There was no way she'd come down this way and risk getting her all white outfit dirty–especially going around the back of the building to walk up from the opposite exit towards the square. No, she was hoping to have a moment with him. A moment alone.

I boiled at the thought. She was after the same man I was. And since Colby hasn't spoken to her since the dinner, she clearly thought she still had a chance with him.

Because he didn't say otherwise.

My knees felt like they may buckle, but there was no way I'd let her see me vulnerable, even though my heart felt like it was a crumbled cookie.

Colby didn't close that door. She could still walk right in.

At this point, I wasn't sure who I was angrier with–Emma or Colby. Emma was just doing what any woman wanting a man would do; she was trying to get him back. Colby was the one who should've closed that door and locked it firmly after the dinner party. He should've stepped up, and he didn't. If I weren't still backed up against this brick wall, I know I'd collapse under the weight of this truth.

Colby didn't tell Emma he wanted me and not her.

I cleared my throat, looking towards the swirl of people, dizzyingly walking by at the square, longing to be anywhere but here. Emma huffed when I didn't make a remark.

"You are sneaky, aren't you? Didn't you know? Colby's father has practically offered Colby's hand in marriage to me. Once this silly little festival of yours is over, Mr. Jackson will have no problem convincing Colby to agree."

My heart thudded. I could feel the panic escalating my magic to near-blowing proportions. It needed to escape, and I needed to keep it in check.

"This isn't the 1800s anymore, Emma. Colby would never agree to an arranged marriage."

Emma lifted her hand to inspect her brightly colored, red fingernails and acted as though she was on top of the world with a knowing that I was not privy to.

"No of course not, I'm not some barbarian. But he and I were good together. We were always good together. He will come to his senses and choose sophistication and class over..." Emma waved her hand vaguely in my direction.

"Whatever *this* is." Emma didn't even wait for a retort, although I was so dumbstruck I don't think I'd come up with something clever enough anyways. The clicking of her heels receded until I could no longer see her. I stood there like a snowman, and couldn't bring myself to move. Every good feeling, every bit of determination I had moments ago, was now completely gone.

Only anger replaced it.

Sparkles began to fall from my palms, and I did my best to calm my racing mind, rubbing on my clothes, nobody will know the difference between the sparkles within the fabric of my uniform or the sparkles from my magic. But despite my best efforts, I couldn't stop the rage and heartbreak I felt. Emma knew she was going to win Colby, had his own dad on her side, and even had experience with him far longer than I had. She *knew* him. Perhaps more than I ever would. I was nothing more than a cute fling in her eyes; she wasn't even intimidated by the fact she saw Colby pressing me against a wall for several minutes. It didn't phase her. She still knew she'd find a way to make him be with her.

This single thought was the icing on the cake.

Turning to the square, I walked at an increasingly fast pace. When I got back to the main street, I frantically scanned the area for Emma. She stood nearby, standing beneath the most glorious ammo: the canopy of the local boutique's tent, *which was covered with snow.* Going beside myself, a haze cast over my usual ability to overlook cruelty–and seeing I was clear of any unwanted eyes–I wiggled my fingers just enough to let those built-up sparkles and energy release. A swirl of power skidded through the chilly air and hit its mark, snapping the edge of the canopy off its poles and barreling downwards, the pile of snow falling directly on top of Emma's ridiculous hat.

Emma screamed, desperately attempting to brush the snow off her clothes, and I couldn't help but laugh at the sight of it. Satisfaction replaced the anger for a brief second, until Emma looked up from under her snow-covered fur monstrosity and saw me laughing at her plight. Her eyes narrowed and she balled her hands into fists.

"YOU! You did this!"

I looked around and put my hands in the air sarcastically. She clearly hadn't heard Colby's remark earlier about my true nature; therefore, she would never know it's me who forced the snow to drop on her head.

"Me? I'm wayyyy over here, Emma. Must've been an unlucky coincidence. It was, however, funny to witness."

Emma seethed as she stomped in a circle, ignoring the boutique owners desperately trying to fix the canopy cover again. She bent down, struggling at first with her gigantic coat puffing awkwardly around her knees, and grabbed a handful of snow. Packing it together, she turned back to me and threw the snowball in my direction.

There's no way she'll hit me.

But I fully underestimated Emma's abilities. She had an arm on her! The snowball came whirling through the air and smacked me directly in the face–**hard.** I slipped and fell bottom-first on the cold ground in front of everybody. A small group of patrons who now heard the commotion, all stood in attention as they wondered what I would do next. But red blurred my vision. I pulled myself back to my feet and armed myself with a snowball of my own making, imbued with my magic, making sure it always hits its mark, and a little extra bite, making it colder than usual.

I threw my ball and hit her square in the chest, knocking her off her feet too. Nobody around us knew whether to help us or to leave us be. And at this point, I wasn't one to usually make a scene, but this girl had gotten under my skin in more ways than one, and I don't think a little snow will cause that much damage.

Emma rolled over and began crawling along the ground towards another booth, where the teenage boys were assisting with the local food shelter for extra credit. They looked sideways at Emma, but when she popped up again, fumbling around in her pocket for her wallet, she handed each boy a 10$ bill. All 4 of them ducked behind the counter.

Oh boy. Ginger, what have you started?

I temporarily spun on my feet, looking around, a sweet, familiar face greeting me from a few steps away. I made my way to stand beside Annie, who had a bag filled to the brim with purchases from the day.

"Ginger! Sweet girl, this is absolutely fabulous! Ohh, Everly would have been so awestruck by what you've done here. My sister loved the holidays, and you have really made this first event such a thrill!"

I smiled at her, wanting not to be rude, but I kept my eyes on the booth Emma hid behind, wondering what devious plan she had up her ridiculous sleeve. Annie was more than perceptive.

"Ginger, have I caught you at a bad time?"

Groaning, I shook my head to say no, but when she cocked her eyebrow at me suspiciously, I relented.

"Well...I may have...not-so-accidentally, pissed off Emma, and now she's retaliating so I'm trying to keep an eye on her."

Annie turned around and noticed the same poofy hat pop out from behind the stand, whispering down to the teenage boys at the booth, and when Annie returned her attention to me, she set down her bag in the snow and began rolling her sleeves up.

"Ooh, don't tell me that. That girl has always rubbed me the wrong way. If you made her mad, you should make her madder."

I couldn't help but smile at the woman; she may not know me well, but gosh, did she treat me like she did.

"You don't like Emma? It seems like Mr. Jackson can only sing high praises of her."

Annie began cracking her knuckles like she was about to start a downright street brawl, and for a moment, I wondered if I should be worried.

"Emma is a nice girl on the surface, but she will chew anyone up and spit them out in a heartbeat. She may be what my esteemed brother-in-law deems worthy, but I, on the other hand, find her as repulsive as a Goosefish."

Although I was confused as to the creature Annie referred to, I could only assume it wasn't the most appetizing thing in the world.

When I finally saw Emma and the 4 teenagers come back up, their arms were filled with dozens of snowballs, and each teen looked like they were ready for war. Emma shrugged off her coat and hung it neatly over the counter of the booth. The boys yelled a literal war cry and began launching the snowballs at me with fierce precision. I, along with several others, ducked and attempted to shield ourselves from the attack, but these boys were good. I caught a glance of Emma, and she wore a smug smile, which only ignited the fire inside me.

Annie covered her arms over her head and yelled at me.

"Move, girl! They are ambushing us!"

We both darted behind the nearby statue of what I assumed to be a previous, famous mayor of Everly Cove, and took cover. Annie clutched her bag to herself, looking at me with determination.

"Ginger, it is your duty to teach that little brat a lesson!"

Before I could respond, Annie was strapping her bag over her shoulder across her chest like she was ready for battle. Gathering a handful of snow, she formed a perfect snowball. She leaned out from behind the statue just enough, and threw the ball of ice directly at one of the teens, knocking him down. She shouted in achievement and glanced back at me, clearly wondering why I hadn't taken her distraction to get going. I nodded at her silently and crawled my way towards the clocktower nearby and hid myself.

With more magic, I quickly created more snowballs and lined them in a row for easier pickup. To my surprise, dozens of other people were forming their own ammo and sending them skyrocketing towards Emma, who screamed and ducked back behind her fort.

Everyone thinks this is part of the event! I can use this to my advantage!

I tucked my snowballs under my arm, and army-crawled around the statue to the line of fir trees. Many people were still debating which to take home for Christmas. Weaving and bobbing my way around people and trees, I looked to the side to see that even more people had joined the pretend fight, and giggles and grunts of hit targets were now echoing around the town square. The teenage boys on Emma's team were now taking a more frontal assault, but two of them were already on other targets: another group of shrieking teen girls who very obviously turned to a flirty match rather than competitive. I could no longer see Annie, but assumed she was among the other participants now joining in. But the other two teens and Emma were now nowhere in sight; in my distraction, I slammed into a hard body.

Colby.

He caught me and patted my shoulders checking to see if I was alright.

"Hey! Ginger! Are you good?"

I hid behind him and looked around suspiciously; part of me yearned to kiss him again. But the other remembered Emma's words, and Colby's lack of communication to his ex. Again, my magic hummed with fury, and I looked up at him with contempt.

"Yeah, Colby. I'm fine."

Colby quirked his head in confusion, and held me in place, pulling my attention back to him.

"Woah, what's going on? Did I do something?"

I refused to make eye contact, otherwise I might lose my edge on Emma and the boys. They were making a move, and I needed to be ready.

"It's what you didn't do, Colby. You seemed to *forget* to inform Emma that you were no longer interested in her. She saw us kissing. And she swears she knows you two will still be together."

His brows furrowed, and he let his hand drop to hold mine. An open act of affection, although the way we were hidden within these trees, I doubt anybody could see.

"Emma is lying, Ginger. I told her the day after the dinner party. But she's relentless. Whatever she said to you isn't true. You have to believe me."

There was a sincerity in his voice that made my heart clench harder. I wanted to believe him. I wanted him to have proclaimed he didn't want that snake of a woman anymore. Yet the confidence in Emma's words made it hard to understand. How could she be so confident she'd end up with Colby if he'd told her to back off?

I finally looked at Colby, it was indeed a dangerous tactic seeing as I was currently engaged in a brawl and I'd already lost sight of my enemy, but it was the only way to truly gauge if he was being genuine. To look into those honey eyes and see it for myself. Worry etched his usually undisturbed features; he was looking nervous, of all things, like he really didn't know if I'd take his word for it or not. *He cared for my opinion of him.*

"If it's true, then why does Emma think she is going to have some crazy arranged marriage with you? The way she speaks is so sure, Colby. She says your dad is planning everything."

Colby's concern turned to outrage.

"She said, what?! Will my father never quit? I told them both, the very next morning after you went to the café, and I went to the town hall, that their games and schemes needed to stop. I was never going to be with Emma again, and the two of them needed to let me live my life. Emma even fake-cried, and my dad comforted her. It was a whole thing, Ginger. I wasn't going to make the same mistake twice by letting you think for a second I ever wanted to be with her."

Looking up at him with surprise, and still a bit of uneasiness, I shrugged my shoulders.

"Why didn't you tell me about this? Maybe I wouldn't have started a freaking snowball war with your ex just now if I'd known she was bluffing!"

Colby looked me up and down, and saw I was still looking around in anticipation, at last realizing why I'd hidden myself in the trees this way. He didn't say anything, but busted out in the biggest laugh I'd ever heard from him. He was literally laughing at me. The whole hands clutching the stomach kind of laugh, can't breathe kind of laugh, *tears forming in his eyes kind of laugh.* I stood there completely defiant, and appalled he'd find this situation so funny when he–in a roundabout way–caused it in the first place! When he finally caught his breath, he tutted his tongue, suggesting I'd been a bad girl. The one he often did in the bedroom that I adored. But right now, it just pisses me off.

"Wait, let me get this straight. Emma told you she was still going to be with me, and you threw a snowball at her?"

I crossed my arms and shook my head.

"No. I dumped a canopy of snow on her head. *She* threw the first snowball if you really want to get technical about it…"

His eyes widened even more in surprise.

"You dumped a canopy of snow on her head?? With what, your magic? Ginger…you are definitely going on the naughty list this year."

His tone was suggestive, but I wouldn't let him distract me.

"She even paid some teenagers to gang up on me! And now a lot of the patrons are participating. Luckily, I think they believe it's part of the event. But she and the boys are missing now, and I know they are coming up with some game plan to sneak attack me."

Colby couldn't help but laugh again.

"Ginger, you're not serious, right? They aren't sneaking around trying to—"

His words cut off mid-sentence the moment a hurtling snowball hit him in the side of the face. I pulled him down quickly behind another tree, and we sat against it, huffing in adrenaline. I peeked around to see the brown-haired boy snap his fingers; clearly, Colby wasn't his target, and his aim was off.

But where was Emma?

Colby wiped the snow off his glasses slowly, turning to me. His eyes glowed with renewed purpose. He now saw the seriousness of our situation.

"Okay. This is war. How can I help?"

I looked at him and raised my eyebrow the way he usually does.

"You want to help me pelt your ex-girlfriend with a snowball?"

He bit his lip excitedly.

"Oh, absolutely, Cupcake."

18

Dinner & A Show

Colby

There may not be many things I know for certain, but there is one: this is by far the best Beef Wellington I've ever made in my life.

As I lift the tray out of the oven and place it neatly on the countertop, I admire my craftsmanship. It was an ode to the cake Ginger made for the business party, expertly topped with snowflake decorations within the pastry wrapping the succulent meat I acquired from the local butcher shop earlier this afternoon. My mom would be so proud of me for getting back in the kitchen.

It's been so long since I cooked like this, I wondered if I'd been too bold to claim I had this incredible surprise for Ginger in the first place. My mom was the one who taught me to cook when I was just 4 years old. I remember watching her make this exact dish, how she took such care to always create some sort of image or decoration on the pastry. One year, she even adorned it with a dinosaur–that year's toddler obsession. I always helped make the mashed potatoes, as they were the best mashed potatoes in the world. She taught me which herbs to use to enhance the flavor and richness, which knives were used for what purpose, and so much more. I credit her for instilling a love of cooking that inspired me to travel the world in search of new flavors, new recipes and bolder concoctions.

I could've made Ginger any exotic dish tonight, but instead, I wanted something closer to home. Something that showed her that she didn't just bring renewed joy to the town, but to my life. She reminded me what was important, and I wanted to give her that in a Christmas gift of my own making as a thank you; a thank you for taking this cold heart and bringing warmth back to my outlook. In more ways than one, Ginger gave me the courage to pursue my passion again. Inspired by her love of baking and putting good food into the bellies of good people, I once again have been eyeing my lonely kitchen. The one I used to toil for hours in trying to create the next best thing, was now calling my name once more, and it felt good to feel at home again.

Walking the Wellington to the dining table, I placed it as the centerpiece in between my mother's favorite set of Christmas dishes, green and gold plates with intricate trees in the center in artistic swirls. Memories of eating on these exact plates welled in my mind as I stepped back to admire the scene. In all the years I've lived in this little house, I haven't hosted a single person. That was always my mom's thing, and doing it myself always brought up the sad reminder that she wouldn't be attending a gathering even if I did one. Now, I was filled with happiness, because she would've still said I didn't know which fork went closest to the plate, and I would still say, "It's just a fork, Mom."

It felt like after so long, my mom's spirit was with me. I only hoped she was proud. Proud that I was finally breaking down my barriers and letting another person into my life–a person I cared for deeply.

Ginger was that person, and there was no better way in my opinion to tell her just that.

The chiming of the doorbell alerted me to the fact that Ginger finally arrived; the moment of truth was here.

Zeus bounded up and down in excitement; he too, has grown accustomed to Ginger being around. Zeus may be friendly with everyone, but Ginger elated him, and showed him the same affection I always have. He'd never grown close to someone the way he has Ginger, and surprisingly, that little fur-demon, Gimli, was now starting to spend time *alone* with Zeus. Yesterday, during the ice sculpture contest, Gimli was walking alongside Zeus all on his own; I even winked at Ginger from across the field of competitors hacking away with their tools as ice chips flung about, and she nodded in appreciation of the newly bonded creatures.

Zeus was already at the door barking when I opened it to find a flushed-faced Ginger, wearing a red sweater with the word "Merry" embroidered on the chest, and a small black mini-skirt with see-through black tights. And lo and behold, black knee-high boots!

She blushed at me after giving some love to Zeus, who walked back inside with Gimli close behind to show him his newest chew toy; Gimli seemed to feign interest.

"What? You're staring at me like I have a glowing red nose on my face."

I shook my head and leaned down to softly kiss her lips.

"No, Cupcake. I'm staring at you like you're the sexiest thing I've ever seen. There's a difference."

She returned the kiss and walked past me, rolling her eyes.

"Mhm, yeah okay. So, tell me, what's this big surprise anyways–"

Ginger gasped. I closed the front door behind me and turned with my hands in the pockets of my grey slacks, my tan turtle neck lifting slightly at my hips as I sheepishly waited for her reaction. Despite the confidence I had in my cooking, would it be enough to please her? Enough to show the effort? Her hand went to clutch her chest, and when I slowly came from behind to check if she was still breathing, she spoke so quietly I almost couldn't hear her.

"Colby...you did...all of this for me?"

As if in a trance, she walked dreamily towards the fully decorated dining table and tears formed in her eyes.

Shit. I didn't just surprise her, I upset her somehow!

I continued standing there, waiting for something, any sign of what was going through her mind. Until she leaned over the table and took a large whiff of the Beef Wellington, inspecting the design along the casing. I cleared my throat, finally bucked up the courage to speak.

"Uh...do you...not like it? I'm sorry if it's too over-the-top, I thought you would enjoy it."

Ginger lifted a finger in the air shushing me.

"Don't you dare apologize. It's perfect. I can't believe you did all this for me."

I shrugged my shoulders in confusion.

"Did what? Cooked for you? That's the basics, Cupcake. You love food, baking, I know–but food in general. I wanted to show you how you inspired me to get back into it. You have done so much for me, and the town; a meal in return is a basic thank you."

She shook her head, wiping a single tear from her cheek, and my heart worried.

"No..." Her voice wavered momentarily. "It's not basic to me. My whole life, I was the cook. The one who fed my family, and not once did anyone else cook *just for me*. I didn't realize it was something I craved so much, until I saw all of this. I didn't know I also craved to be surprised. Be taken care of. Why? Why did you do all this? It's so incredible, Colby!"

Her delight at the meal made my heart settle, all the nerves while prepping and setting up fading immediately. I smiled at her as she covered her mouth in awe, staring at the table, and walked to stand behind her, my arms wrapping tightly around her shoulders in a hug. Resting my chin on the top of her head, I whisper softly.

"Because, you made me feel whole again, Ginger. You brought so much light and happiness back to town, and...my life. I wanted to show you that you also deserve someone doing something nice for you."

She leaned against my chest and I breathed in her scent, a mixture of peppermint and sage; a delicate balance that made me feel as though I was finally home again. Not desiring to be anywhere else in the world, not wanting to run away–but at last stay put, and savor the moment with someone. I whispered again, brushing her hair back behind her shoulders, luxuriating in the soft texture of those curls that I have come to adore.

"But, it is best eaten warm, so let's say we have a true date and sit together to eat, hm?"

Ginger came out of her mid-trance and looked up at me.

"Is that what this is? A date?"

Raising my eyebrow at her, I nodded casually.

"What? Did you truly think I wasn't a gentleman at all?"

With one hand on the small of her back, I guided her to a seat and pulled at the chair dramatically, bow and all. She chuckled and took a seat, doing an extra flourish of patting down her skirt like she was wearing something fit for a queen.

"I do suppose I suspected you weren't the type to wine and dine a woman with the state of that poor couch of yours..."

I threw my hands over my mouth in shock.

"Hey, now! That couch is a classic, and just because I have a well-worn and loved couch, doesn't mean I have zero sophistication. Comfort is key on a couch I hoped we'd end up on after this very *classy* meal."

I winked sarcastically at her while taking the opposite seat, I grabbed the bottle of red wine I'd sat nearby, unstopping the cork, pouring us each a generous glass.

"Excuse me! I forgot that you *definitely* knew how to woo a woman–feed her and then take her to the peeling leather couch–Oh yes, how romantic."

Shrugging my shoulders, I slice open the Beef Wellington, placing a perfectly pink centered piece onto her plate, serving it alongside mashed potatoes and the asparagus I'd made earlier.

"What can I say? You wouldn't like me much if I was all one way or the other; you tend to have favored that couch as our nightly meeting spot on more than one occasion—romance still included. A bit of grit with your romance is always a cherry on top. How else would I make you squirm for me the way I do? Who told you that romance can't involve a good throwing over the couch at the end?"

She blushed, and instantly, the heat rose within my body, remembering having done that exact thing the last night we were together. She was insatiable, the absolutely perfect combination of fire and sweetness wrapped into a Ginger-sized present just for me, and I wished to unwrap her each and every night I could.

"Is this how you've always been? This interesting combination of Scrooge and Prince Charming?"

Once plating hers, I grabbed a plentiful helping for myself and looked over to Gimli already snoozing on the floor nearby, Zeus playing happily with his latest toy.

"Well, if you're asking if I've always been this good in the romance department, then no—it has never felt this easy with someone before. Usually women are not so intrigued by the sour then sweet package I typically come in."

Ginger took a bite of the food, making the most intoxicating "Mmmm" sound, and my heart triple-flipped at the satisfaction on her face.

"Okay, minor change of subject because, Colby, this is the best food I've ever tasted!"

I tried to hide my excitement at her praise, but I smiled and looked down at my own plate.

"I'm glad you like it."

She took another mouthful alongside the mashed potatoes before continuing.

"So, back to before, you had a hard time with ladies then?"

Nodding, I wiped my mouth and took another sip of wine before responding.

"Are you calling me unlucky? Or that I have a knack for picking emotionally unavailable women?"

The reference was toward Emma of course, who I'd already told Ginger had the emotional capacity of a rock. A very painted-up rock–but a rock, nonetheless. Ginger smiled as she tilted her wine glass, the red of it accentuating the red of her lipgloss, and I had to avert my eyes to keep from going to wicked places.

"Maybe. Though, I do find it hard to believe anyone would run from–" She paused looking me up and down like I was actually the decadent meal of the evening and not the one I cooked. "*This*. Unless you're hiding skeletons in your closet, then I think we need to have a talk."

Ginger laughed at her own joke, and although it was funny, there was a delicate truth behind her question. I cut through a bite of the meat, but paused midway, my mind beginning to think back on all the reasons other relationships in the past didn't work. Regrettably, I could feel the playful mood shift within me.

"Not literally, but I think looking back, I never made space for anyone intimately like that. I was always too serious, too closed off–even before my mother passed. But after that? It was like I couldn't trust anyone with my softer side."

Ginger put her own fork down and looked at me with those stunning eyes.

"But, you want to?"

This was a question I never considered before: if I actually *wanted* to let my guard down, let someone in completely to know all the sharp edges and the complexities. To know the sides of myself I often hid, or batted away like an annoying fly pestering me to acknowledge.

Did I truly want to give myself entirely to someone?

When her eyes filled with understanding, she reached across the table and held my hand, squeezing it reassuringly. That's when it all clicked into place–the answer to her question.

I do want to give myself to someone. But not just anyone.

Only her.

Looking down between our hands, I knew exactly what I wanted. This time, I would give it my all, because there would never be another Ginger, never another who could come in like a glitter bomb of chaos and fulfill me the way she has.

I met her eyes again and rubbed the top of her thumb, her gaze transitioning from comfort to mirror her own deep, unresolved feelings. She hesitated, her words barely audible as she spoke, her eyes still holding mine like a captive.

"You know, when you look at me like that, I forget why I'm not supposed to fall for you."

This admission was all I needed. The last piece to the puzzle. I stood and walked to the other side of the table, pulling her to her feet as I pushed the dishes aside. She let me hoist her up onto the table; never for a second did I take my eyes off hers. The atmosphere around us was electrifying as my thumb ran over her delicate lips, teasingly.

"Then stop trying to, Ginger."

I kissed her as deeply as I could, her hands quickly finding their way up my arms, trailing her nails lightly along them, causing my pulse to race. My hands gripped her thighs, all of me coming undone between her lips. I didn't know if it was the fusion of desire and tenderness, or the way she held onto me–acting like she never wanted me to let her go–but I was unfurling further with each second.

Between breathless pauses, my adrenaline was coursing and all reason was being left behind. Swallowing hard to steady myself, I pull back only enough to get the words out.

"This–whatever this is between us, isn't temporary for me. The question you asked earlier...I want that. *All of it*. And the moment I say these words out loud–the ones tearing me absolutely apart–I'll make damn sure you never forget them. I'm not letting you go. Not for anyone. Not even the North Pole, Cupcake."

I watched in agony as she studied my expression, clearly gauging the severity level of my admission. As her lips parted, I knew she felt the same, and as I closed the gap, ready to kiss her again after I told her she was all I wanted and more, her Spiritometer buzzed along the dining table. Not once. *Twice*.

Her eyes glanced towards the device with the worst timing on the planet. I grabbed her face to return her attention to me, but I could feel the moment fleeting, and my resolve dissipating. Sighing, I kissed her softly, whispering against her lips.

"You should see who that is."

Guilt riddled her face, but she reached over to pick it up and looked at the screen, her expression turning to pure horror.

"Is everything okay?"

She shakes her head and clutches her phone to her chest, her eyes filled with a worry and fear I didn't understand. Not that I understood everything about her predicament or Elf business, as she'd been incredibly open, but I continued to feel there was something she wasn't letting on about. Finally, she met my gaze and bit her bottom lip the way she does when she's anxious.

"Um, yeah. Everything is okay, but I need to go right now. Elf stuff...I'm so sorry we couldn't finish. But this was the most special night, thank you."

Before I could even respond, she was kissing me sweetly and calling for Gimli, who was already out of the door again into the winter night.

I turned and grabbed the wine, taking a generous helping straight from the bottle, still staring at the door as if sheer will power could turn her back around. Zeus let out a soft whimper on his spot he'd made on the rug, the sound of it reflecting my own defeated heart.

19

Sister Showdown

Ginger

When I arrive at my cottage, the lights inside are already on, a figure standing with arms crossed in the window.

It's my sister.

A snowstorm unleashes in my stomach, and even though she's my own sibling, I've never been more scared of someone in my life. She is the person who has forced me under a shadow I never knew had a lifetime expectancy. Clara is the one who I was always striving harder because of, working longer hours in spite of, and still coming up short for any type of compliment from her. We may be in the same department in the North Pole, but she was a manager. She climbed to that role so fast, she's been put in the *Santa's Helpers Hall of Fame* for the youngest field officer with the most success in raising Spirit levels in over 50 places around the world.

She's good, and she knows it. And she makes it a point to remind me ad-nauseam every time we are together. I always thought growing up, how much fun it would be to work alongside one of my siblings; my two younger have such sweet countenance and personalities; we adore every moment of time we have together. But Clara is the exact opposite, we have never been able to get along–*especially* at work.

The last time I corresponded with her was when Colby's sweet Aunt Annie said she'd personally deliver my letter for me. I hadn't even received a letter in return from her, and even Izabelle had gone so far as to ask if I'd heard anything from Headquarters.

I guess a letter wouldn't suffice for whatever this must be.

I braced myself and went up the few steps to the cottage doorway. Once the handle was in my grasp, I took a deep breath before walking inside the warmed, cozy house. Dropping my coat at the rack by the front door, I walked through the domed archway that led to the small living space.

My sister continued to look out the window, not bothering to turn my way or offer a friendly greeting. I felt like I did when I was a little girl, needing to go have a conversation with my parents again for misusing my ability to speak with animals to gain a better advantage to all the North Pole secret passageways. This was when I refused to believe I couldn't become a baker one day, and kept trying to find places to secretly practice in the kitchens around the Pole. Clara always maintained this same way to deal with difficult situations, more often than not, when I was in trouble for a work thing that could cause people to frown against her or the Tinsel legacy.

Gimli was following me inside after I'd carried him in my bag on the trip over to avoid the snow. For a cat who grew up in one of the coldest and snowiest places on the planet, the little ball of fur detested getting wet from snow. He quickly found his way to my lap, and settled himself in a seated position, eyeing Clara like he was debating on whether or not he should go claw up her perfectly pressed suit pants already or not.

Clara wore a fitted, deep maroon suit with a matching jacket and flared pants. Her feet were covered by black, modest heels, and her hair was neatly placed in a low bun at the base of her neck. Unlike me, whose hair always looked untamed–with precarious curls that stubbornly fell about my face–Clara's hair was slicked back with precision.

She was the picture of elegance, severity, and bound by order in all things. Whereas I was the picture of clumsiness and getting by on my instincts, more easily able to come up with clever– albeit sometimes *creative*–solutions. There has never been a time in my life when we agreed on anything, and there was no feeling of wanting a sisterly hug or embrace; not when she stood there like a judge ready to strike me down for my transgressions.

When minutes passed and all that fell between us was heavy breaths, I finally cleared my throat.

"Clara, tell me what brings my big sister down here? Are you here to congratulate me on what a spectacular job I've done in Everly Cove? If so, I'm ready for whatever award you've deemed I'm finally capable of winning."

Sarcasm dripped from every word, and I knew it wasn't necessarily the correct approach with my sister, but I knew if she was here, whatever it was, it wouldn't be in my favor. Where's the harm in masking my fear with a bit of disdain and heavy-handed smack talk?

Clara unfolded her arms and spun around slowly, taking a seat in the chair opposite me. Gimli angled his head and meowed something I dared not utter to my sister. She rolled her eyes, scowling in Gimli's direction.

"I don't know what rude remark he has for me today, but, no need to repeat it. I'm sure it's a mixture of mocking my "Old lady clothes" and "Why don't you go off somewhere where the Yetis live and get taken for a few days so we don't need to suffer your snobbery.""

I had to restrain myself from laughing. Indeed, she was spot on. But actually, Gimli mentioned more particularly how that color did nothing for my sister's complexion and asked if she had some children's dreams to destroy by sending out strongly worded rejection memos, stating they wouldn't be on Santa's Good List this year.

Although they weren't necessary comments, the jeers from my fussy feline did ease my anxiety. He did it more for me than for anyone else; he always knew his humor made me feel more battle ready, especially around Clara. Unfortunately, she also knew Gimli well and was always ready for whatever comments he'd bring to the table. Gimli did his equivalent of a grunt and settled himself to lie in my lap, letting me pet his head slowly to calm myself.

Clara picked a piece of lint off her shoulder before opening her own Spiritometer, but hers was handed out to higher-level agents and included entry to our entire database on agents in the field, mission details, and more. Scrolling her thumb over it briefly, she breathed loudly, vexation now at its peak.

"Despite you or your unruly cat's attitude towards me, I think you should have some idea as to why I'm here. And no, it's not for a reward, Ginger. It's far worse than that."

I feared I wouldn't be able to swallow from how tight my throat felt at her words. I tried my best to stay quiet, not wanting to 'out' myself in case she was talking of something else...but the way she stared me down, like I'd taken away the biggest promotion of her life—told me she knew everything already. But there was no way I'd admit to anything yet.

"I don't know what you're talking about. Since I've arrived in Everly Cove, I've managed to raise Christmas Spirit levels to 86% now, and brought the townspeople together over a festival and event for a good cause; even Izabelle has seen all the hard work I've put in. Not only in the café, but in the camaraderie of the town. I would say for my first mission, I've done an excellent job. And I know for certain that after tomorrow's Christmas charity ball, we will have the energy we need for the sled, the reindeer, and the presents to take off as planned, bringing cheer and goodwill to all the children of the world. Just like every year before."

Clara *laughed*.

Actually laughed out loud for the first time I may have heard in years. But this laugh was not jovial; it was filled with condescension. I never would've predicted this reaction.

"Okay, great. You manage to bring Spirit levels up and might save Christmas. But you managed to expose our world, our way of life, and everything we hold dear...to a **human**, Ginger. Everything you've accomplished here will vanish in the blink of an eye because you couldn't shield yourself from the humans. Not to mention...*actually date one.*"

Everything inside me turned into a ball of mush. My biggest fear of discovery was now out in the open, and there was nothing I could do to deny. How could she know about all of this?

"I only exposed myself because I nearly fell off a cliff into the ocean! I had to use my dust to help me, and in the rulebook it says it's permissible to use in case of emergency. Would you not consider losing my life an *emergency*, Clara?"

"I would if you hadn't decided to go out into a snowstorm at night along a cliff in the first place." Her tone was firm, but not shocked by my revelation of how I exposed myself to Colby.

I wrinkled my nose in confusion.

"How in the sugar plums do you even know about that?"

Clara didn't look at me, and for a split second, I almost saw a hint of regret in her eyes.

"I sent another agent to keep tabs on you."

"You mean Izabelle? But she's been with me the whole time and she doesn't know about Colby seeing me."

Just as the words fell out of my mouth, I heard a rustle of a leather jacket behind me.

Izabelle was standing cross-legged in the doorframe towards the kitchen, having been hidden by the dim lighting. She didn't look angry, but her expression was filled with disappointment and even sadness; sadness for never confiding in her when we'd grown so close over the last weeks. She may be a hard candy cane on the outside, but she was actually a soft, caring friend. One I secretly was so grateful to have on this journey, and one I had come to think of as a *best* friend. Izabelle has put up with my shenanigans and crazy ideas this entire time, with only support and validation for my efforts. Now looking into those dark, near-black irises, I saw the betrayal from not telling her about Colby–or how far our relationship has gone.

I picked up Gimli, who mewed at me before conceding and taking a seat on the floor beside me. I stood to face Izabelle and hugged my arms around myself as I spoke.

"Izabelle...I'm so sorry you had to find out this way. I knew my exposure was already going to get me in trouble, and I didn't want to risk you getting caught in the chestnut roasting fire alongside me. I *wanted* to tell you. About the exposure. About Colby and I–about all of it. I didn't know how to without causing more damage."

Izabelle remained silent, hearing my words with understanding, but a pain struck her features in a way that only made the racking guilt worse.

"You should've told me, Ginger. But I understand and appreciate you trying to protect me. There's something you need to understand though. When Clara asked me to come here, I knew this was no ordinary mission. From the stories I'd heard about you–I knew you were no *ordinary* Elf. I wanted to help, in every way, because when I watched your enthusiasm at the monthly departmental meeting, it inspired me to want to be a part of it. It wasn't just because I owed your sister for a scrape she'd gotten me out of years ago, so I came here. I took the assignment with you because I thought together, we could save Everly Cove. I already had my suspicions of you and Colby. Unlike the rest of the Pole, I do not share the same sentiment that being involved with a human is bad."

She paused, and either by trick of the light or a figment of my imagination, she wiped the corner of her eye before stiffening back to her usual manner to hide the brief emotion I didn't think I'd see from her.

"I only wish you'd come to me so I could've helped you further. We're...friends. *Good friends*. At least, that's how I have come to feel. I wish you hadn't held onto all this fear of the repercussions alone."

Before she even finished her last sentence, I was already rushing to pull her in for a hug. I was so relieved when she relented, hugging me in return.

"Oh, Izabelle! Thank you! We are good friends, and I wish I had told you earlier, too."

When I turned back to Clara, she looked a bit stunned by Izabelle's response; clearly she didn't think we would get so close during this mission, but she only let it momentarily phase her before her stern expression returned. The outrage at the realization of her previous statement finally clicked into place.

"You sent an agent *other than Izabelle*. To spy on us. ***On me***."

Clara adjusted in her seat uncomfortably at my harsh tone.

"Yes, I did. I never agreed to put you on this mission. You've never been on any other assignment, and this is the biggest one we've faced in hundreds of years. There was no way you had enough experience for this. But for whatever reason, my boss decided to give it to *you*, of all Elves. I sent one of my own special operatives undercover as one of the local business owners, I believe he chose the role of the local grocer, and therefore, he was there at the Business Banquet, the festival activities, and even saw how close you got to this human, Colby—even after your exposure to him on the cliffside. He's been corresponding with me for the entirety of the last few weeks, and the moment I saw how far you let it go on, I knew there was nothing better to do but come down here to make sure you understand what's going to happen next."

In all my years, I never felt the urge to sling some of my magic at my sister more than I do right now. My insides were knotted garland, jabbing me with each racing thought in my head that tried to unravel the prickly feeling of defeat and rage within me. Still, there was no denying—this is the worst I've ever felt in regards to my sister. She never trusted me for this mission. She didn't think I was responsible enough to handle it.

But she was only half right. I had successfully managed my mission parameters. And Colby...it's not like I came here looking to fall in love.

Love.

Because for the first time, I could admit it to myself. In the prospect of losing everything I've worked so hard for on this mission, and knowing I'd lose him...the recognition of what he came to mean to me, my feelings welled up inside me. There was no denying it.

I love Colby Jackson. More than I've ever loved another soul.

I only wish I'd come to realize it sooner. Like earlier, when I was pinned against his body on the dining table, and the tensions rose to the point *he almost said it to me.* At least, so much of me longed to hear it from him, despite how afraid I was. If my sister hadn't interrupted one of the most romantic and significant moments of my life, Colby and I could very well be making love, whispering it continuously to each other until we fell into a fit of giggles. Then, I'd kiss him even more, relishing in knowing we were together, and that's all that mattered.

But it would be a lie, because so much more was at stake than a promise of something he wouldn't remember after tomorrow.

My sister finally stood, facing me down like a polar bear ready for a brawl. But she kept her composure...

"Here's what will happen. You will go on with your ball, in hopes of gathering the remaining Spirit we need for this mission's success. I will allow you a time to say goodbye to Colby, and immediately after the event, I will proceed with the mind erasing protocol. You will come back home with me to the North Pole for a trial on how to properly deal with your future in the department...*and* the Pole."

Even though I'd imagined what might happen if my exposure to a human was caught, the reality was setting in, and I did all I could to stop myself from crying right there in front of Clara. I wouldn't give her that satisfaction, though. Izabelle continued to stand by my side, holding my hand, clearly attempting to show more friendly gestures. My voice wavered, but I squeezed Izabelle's hand for strength and threw icicles at Clara with my eyes.

"You have never been the kindest sister, but you should've trusted me more. If I agree to your demands, you must let Izabelle get out of this entirely. She didn't know until tonight what had transpired. She is not to be punished for my mistakes."

Clara ticked her eyes between Izabelle and I, throwing her hands in her pocket, ready to have this negotiation over with.

"Of course. She will go unpunished. Happy?"

There was nothing more I could say. Clara flattened out her jacket before giving a curt goodbye.

"I will be attending the ball tomorrow to keep an eye on how the evening goes. See you both then. Have a good rest of your evening."

As Clara closed the front door, Izabelle looked down at me, our hands still joined. Without saying a word, she turned me around for another hug, and I let the tears I'd held back, fall. While I sobbed in my friend's arms, there was only one thought that repeated in my mind:

More than one person would be changed this Christmas, but only one naive Elf's heart would be broken.

20

Yuletide Waltz

Colby

"**D**ude, you look great! Ginger is going to be so impressed with you, and not to mention, the way you've gotten this auditorium to look for the ball...Let's just say, I see the spark in you again, Colby."

My friend Tom beamed at me in the bathroom mirror. Just outside the bathroom was the town hall auditorium he referred to, and he wasn't wrong; even a glimpse of the makeshift ballroom blew me away as Tom ushered me in here to check myself out. He wore a grey suit that had a tail, and he even sported a top hat–believing himself to feel incredibly royal. I thought it might be ridiculous when he mentioned it to me earlier, but in the end, the look worked well for him. He seemed happy, as did everyone else who was seen entering the fully decorated winter wonderland.

I may not have gone so regal in my look, but I do have to admit–I looked *good*. I picked a velvet black suit that reflected the light rather nicely, with a matching bowtie that Tom helped me place. My pants cuffed perfectly at the tops of my shoes that I had kept in a box since I bought them years ago–always seeming too fancy for what I typically wore. But tonight, they matched my suit as if I bought them together, when in reality, the suit was chosen and tailored by my Aunt Annie, who'd begun crying when she saw me arriving at the town hall tonight. I promptly hugged her and shushed her into the room to begin talking with the arrivals.

Knowing that everyone was so thrilled for the event, that ticket sales skyrocketed, and all of it was going toward Dementia relief, for the first time in years, our vibrant little coastal town felt alive again with anticipation. But really, this was only one of the reasons I put so much effort into the ball.

When I offered to take care of it for Ginger, she'd quirked that eyebrow at me like I'd just told her the craziest thing ever. She questioned my abilities to properly create a whimsical and majestic setting that would make everyone feel like kings and queens. I assured her with only a little taunting, and with her being so busy with the other events and preparing for the banquet she had put on for the ball, she agreed. My greatest achievement thus far was how I'd successfully kept her in the dark about what I created in her absence.

Tom gave me another pat on the back as we made our way out of the bathroom. I stopped briefly for another look in the mirror, adjusting the collar of my jacket, and for the first time in years, I looked like myself again–not the stranger who stared back –a ghost perhaps, haunted by the what ifs and the void I felt that overtook my life with my mother's passing. With the courage to step out of the shadows of grief–thanks to a woman who helped me see that missing my mother didn't mean I couldn't find her elsewhere–I felt her presence again, here in this town that adored her and had stood by my side all my life.

Like a fog lifting over the Maine ocean horizon, just at the cusp of morning after a rain, I finally felt like the blur of the last few years of bitterness I latched onto, was also beginning to lift.

All because a quirky, wild-haired, Elf came barreling into my life with a kick of peppermint, sass, and a whole lot of empathy for a Scrooge who didn't think himself or his life worthy. With each time I encountered Ginger, she not only gave me a good reminder that rudeness was not the way to govern my life, but that there are people who care for me in Everly Cove–the very people I didn't need to push away.

They all waited patiently for me to get a bearing on my grief and confusion, all showing up happily, with arms wide open throughout the renewal of this festival. They all quickly forgave my attitude and evasiveness toward my duties with them. The conversations I've had with people this week have changed my life. I've heard so many stories of fun times with my mom, how much they all enjoyed the effort Ginger and I were putting into bringing some light and Christmas joy back, and how proud they were to see me blossoming in the hometown I tried so hard to run from before.

All the while, Ginger stood and regarded me like I was the star upon a Christmas tree, always encouraging me–even when I did my best attempts to avoid it–chatting with as many of my neighbors and new arrivals as possible. She knew I was starved for connection; she knew it without me ever saying a word to her. She knew that I longed to be a part of a community again.

She was stubbornly perceptive that way.

Yet that perceptiveness has given me back so much of what I longed for—*love*. Because by all things infuriating about this woman, she was all I could think of. Dream of. I believe so wholeheartedly that I want her to annoy the ever-loving jingle bells out of me for as long as she will have me.

I know she's been afraid of what will happen once Christmas comes tomorrow. I haven't even had the opportunity to ask if she was staying or leaving. Long distance can be difficult, but I'm pretty sure long distance to the North Pole would be nearly impossible for a human guy who couldn't catch a flight there—as none existed.

But after the failed attempt of telling her my feelings last night, and the rush out the door, I worried I was already losing my chance at letting her know how I felt, and to ask if she'd consider staying with me. Okay, maybe not ask. **Beg**. Hell, I'd stay there with frost-bitten digits if I knew we'd be together.

Is it selfish when I know she's bound by duty in the Pole? Of course it is. But if I had to bribe Santa himself to let me stay there, I'd follow Ginger Tinsel across the globe, to the coldest and most secluded place on Earth, where the wi-fi is probably spotty and the hot cocoa comes out in fountains—basically, my very own Hallmark Christmas movie on steroids.

I'd do it for her, give up my life here in Everly Cove if she couldn't stay. Which is exactly what I will tell her when she arrives tonight. With a final glance, I let out a short breath and readied myself to face whatever came next.

When I arrived back in the ballroom, I was taken aback by the beauty of what a job the town hall custodians did in decorating it.

The auditorium had a second floor atrium, several places with little pockets for seating. I believe the town hall also used to host plays in the early days, so the room resembled an old, grand theater. A staircase wound in a semi-spiral along the right corridor from the balcony which was open to look upon the main floor.

The hardwood floor shined after a fresh waxing, the herringbone pattern accentuating the feeling of elegance underneath the newly cleaned crystal chandelier, which hung from the painted domed ceiling. Colors of light blue and silver illuminated a cloud formation that was painted by a local artist in the 1910s.

Along the walls of the space sat beautiful evergreen trees between every doorway that entered the auditorium, embellished with ornaments of bright silver and icicle blue that glistened in the chandelier light, dotting the room in a mesmerizing way, resembling falling snow under moonlight.

If my father knew what budget I used for this, he'd have my head. But if this was successful, I believe he will be in good graces with the townspeople for the rest of his career. It may have been risky, but he wouldn't mind if it brought him prestige and another run for office.

Perhaps it was all too much, but I wanted to surprise Ginger, because I hoped she'd love it as much as I did.

The room was already filled to the brim with people in ballgowns and suits, the chatter bright and lively. I waved at Izabelle, who was manning the buffet table set on the far wall covered in delicious meats, cheeses, hors d'oeuvres, and dishes fit for a palace. Ginger worked herself to the bone preparing it all the last several days, and it definitely didn't disappoint. She had a gift with food, her pastries and cakes sitting like sculptures along the far end of the table. The talent and artistry of them blew me away. Many were already sampling, and I could hear gasps of delight at the concoctions she created.

Izabelle wore a satin red ball gown, which suited her personality. She nodded in my direction, her nonchalant way of saying hello, and continued to plate for guests.

There was no sign of my father yet as I took a slow turn to inspect the crowd, my heart stopping when my eyes reached the top of the stairs.

Ginger's hazel eyes met mine, and I swore under my breath at the sight of her. She dazzled in a silver gown that flowed like a flower petal. The top of it was lace, dabbled with glitter. Little pearls and beads intertwined in the mesh as they flowed down into off-the-shoulder, sheer sleeves. Her mass of curly red hair was pulled half up in a delicate twist, as the rest fell in waves down her back. Small braids were wrapped around the top of her head to finish the stunning ensemble, like a crown fit for royalty. Nestled within her braids sparkled the same matching pearls woven in her dress.

She's the most captivating thing I've ever seen.

I gave myself a mental pat on the back, seeing as she, unknowingly, matched the aesthetic and misty silver tones I arranged for the evening. Although Ginger mostly wore reds and greens, which always accentuated her gorgeous green eyes or her fiery hair—silver made her look like a goddess descending the stairs, and her green eyes shone brightly against the backdrop.

She looked down at me with a smile that made me feel as though I was the only person in the room. The only person she wanted to see above any other. As she gently lifted the hem of her dress, making her way down the stairs, I stood silently in awe of her until she reached the bottom and stood before me. Clearing my throat, I wondered if I blushed, because she looked at me as though it'd taken me a moment to speak.

"If there was a princess of Everly Cove, you would be it, Cupcake. You look...incredible."

I offered a hand out to her, and she bit her lip out of nervousness, but curtsied and took my offer.

"You sir, look like a duke if I ever saw one. You never told me you cleaned up so well."

Slapping on my signature devil-may-care smile, holding her hand in mine, I began guiding her towards the center of the room where slow dancing had already begun. A live string quartet played Christmas classics in orchestral rhythms that reminded me of those old movies during the holidays I'd watched with both my parents growing up; the movies that shone like nostalgia and the reminder of what the true meaning this time of year brings. Ginger looked around us in awe as I steadily spun her in a circle, causing a laugh that made me feel as light as air.

"Well, princess, if you must know—I only dressed up this much for you."

Ginger's eyes glinted with amusement and doubt; she wrinkled her nose as she placed one hand upon my shoulder, letting me guide her into a classic Waltz, slowly turning us as I held her hand firmly in my own. The closeness, the way she looked at me, the way she shined under the chandelier–I wondered if I could be dreaming. She looked down at our feet a few times, and I laughed.

"Did you think I would have two left feet?"

Ginger smiled at me in a way to say yes.

"You caught me. Have you always been such a lovely dancer?"

Shrugging my shoulders as I twirled her once more, this time pulling her body even closer to me, her eyes swam with the same passion I was feeling.

"Actually no, but my Aunt gave me a few tips earlier this week. Don't ask me too many details, but it resulted in a lot of feet stomping and a lot of embarrassment. And to already answer your next question, it was not my feet that suffered."

Laughter gushed from Ginger as she allowed me to continue gliding her along the floor, trusting me so completely, and I relished the way she so easily put her faith in me this way. Many other couples were already dancing alongside us, and I'm sure the sight of ballgowns and suits in this old auditorium was a wonder to see. Ginger squeezed my hand as she spoke.

"I can't believe you did that to be able to dance with me. You did *all of this*, just for me, didn't you?"

Letting my hand slide along her spine, I pulled her tighter to my chest, my voice nearing a whisper.

"Do...you like it?"

She looked up at me, and for the first time, I noticed tears. I gave a final spin, and Ginger gripped the lapel of my jacket.

"I *love* it. It's absolutely spectacular, the care and detail you brought to life for this event—it's beyond words! Colby...I was meaning to tell you something else, too."

Her face then changed. Her smile faded, and worry etched her features. She sucked in a breath, and a rushing of fear struck my chest, squeezing the air from my lungs in a heartbeat. This couldn't be good.

She's going to end it. She's going to say she doesn't want this anymore, because she's leaving.

Ginger stopped moving, and all at once I thought I might fall right there in the middle of the dance floor. But when she leaned up quickly and kissed me, her hands on the sides of my face pulling me down, she actually kissed me in front of everyone—after all the hiding, after all the talk of the consequences of others knowing we had been together—it all vanished as she finally pulled back, and I couldn't hear the music anymore. Only her soft voice and the words I'd longed to hear for weeks now.

"I love you, Colby. I love you so much. I didn't know being with someone could feel this way, and now... I know, *truly know*—that I love you more than I thought possible. You have changed my life this Christmas, and I need you to know that."

An instant rush of disbelief and pure happiness flooded my body. I grabbed her by the waist and picked her up in the air, spinning her in a circle before dipping her in my arms as I kissed those cherry-red lips to my heart's content. The same lip gloss I've grown to crave, the same way she clasps her arms tightly around my neck, and the words I wasn't sure she would say–this is by far the best night of my life. When I finally broke the kiss and gently brought her back up, she chuckled as I cupped the sides of her face, kissing her forehead, closing my eyes and imprinting this into my memory.

Half breathy, she looked up at me as I finally removed myself.

"I love you, Ginger. You've been a gift, an absolute gift to me. I've been daydreaming of you saying those words for a while, and it did not disappoint. You kept me waiting, Cupcake. I'll be sure to remind you of that for all time."

Ginger's face flushed in guilt.

"I know, I'm so sorry for that. I wanted to tell you last night."

I let my knuckles gently run along her freckled cheek reassuringly.

"Don't apologize, you're telling me here, *now*, it's more than perfect."

She smiled just as the music came back into focus and clapping began for the end of the song. Everyone began gathering around the buffet table to begin eating; round tables were placed on the corners of the room decorated with white table clothes and candles. When Ginger tugged at my hand to follow her, we passed a waiter on the way to the front of the auditorium. She took two of the offered champagne glasses on the waiter's tray, handing me one as we continued towards an object sitting on a table.

Finally, I saw the brown, glaring eyes of my father standing beside the table. I tightened my hold on Ginger's hand, remembering the last encounter I had with him at the festival was a complete disaster, and I would not let him say anything to hurt Ginger again tonight.

Ginger ushered me directly to him, and my insides churned from the unknown of how my father would react. He watched us questioningly, but remained a beacon of calm and collected. Raising his own champagne glass in the air at us as we approached, I did not return the gesture.

"Good evening, you two. That was quite the spectacle-your dance on the floor tonight. I do have to say, Ginger, you have outdone yourself with this event. We haven't had a charity fundraiser this successful in years. I truly appreciate what you've done for the town, and in honor of my dear Everly."

My mouth opened in amazement. My dad was complimenting Ginger; he was *thanking* her. I looked to Ginger to gauge her reaction, but all I saw was a delicate grin.

"Thank you, Mayor Jackson. But this ball was all Colby. He really did an amazing job, and he did every part of it himself. He wanted it to be special for everybody, but most importantly, he believes your wife's honor deserves the best. I appreciate you allowing us to use the town hall for the night."

My dad nodded and looked around the room at the large crowd the night brought.

"This is truly exceptional for Everly Cove, the cheer and atmosphere were the lightest they'd been in years. I don't know how you do it, Ginger, but everyone has taken to you. You have helped bring Everly Cove out of the shadows."

Ginger knocked my shoulder slightly. I finally looked at my dad and agreed. However, I can't help but remain skeptical.

"Yes, in more ways than one. She inspired me to do something, to give back. Like mom always hoped we might someday." I paused and looked around the crowd. "I don't see Emma anywhere, have you two finally accepted my choice, or is she still prepping herself for some grand entrance the two of you planned?"

A sadness washed over his face, and he clutched his champagne glass a little closer to his chest.

"No, there will be no more Emma. She left on an early flight this morning after barging into my office to let me know she gave up, and said if you chose Ginger over her, it was your loss." He waited a moment before continuing, raising an eyebrow at me. "I was told she was beaten by you in a *snowball* fight?"

Ginger covered her mouth to hide her smile as I rolled my eyes.

"She tried to embarrass Ginger, but we ended up winning that war. Maybe that's why she really left, not because she was truly upset we weren't getting back together, but to lick her wounds over a few frozen chunks of snow."

"Yes, I do believe you're right." My dad took another long pause, looking for what to say next. When he looked at us again, his usual rigid demeanor had changed to something casual, more like a father talking to his son rather than a mayor to his constituent.

"I apologize for meddling in your love life. I have only ever wanted what's best for you. But you are a grown man and have always been capable of making your own decisions. As it shows here tonight, the care you have taken to honor your mom...it's truly wonderful. I only wish we could've honored her in such a way sooner, together."

Ginger gave a small cough, and I was unable to speak on either the unusual apology or the 'together' bit of my dad's words. Watching as Ginger sat her glass down on a nearby table, her heels clicked as she stepped away, her dress moving as she swished between the two of us without another word. Izabelle came out from another area behind the table with the hidden object, and handed Ginger a microphone. Tapping it briefly, the entire room fell silent.

"Hi everybody! We are so happy to have you here enjoying Everly Cove's first ever Yuletide Christmas Ball charity event for Dementia Relief!"

Everybody clapped excitedly–even my father. I watched proudly as Ginger gave me a small wink before continuing–my mind still reeling from my father's change of attitude this evening.

"Tonight is a special occasion, a time to bring us all together, but mostly, a night to honor a woman who impacted this community in so many ways. Tonight, we honor Everly Jackson and memorialize her right here in this auditorium for many years to come."

Ginger handed the microphone back to Izabelle and grabbed the large tapestry that disguised the object, lifting it off to reveal an extraordinary portrait of my mother. Painted in oils and bold colors, her likeness was uncanny; with the sparkle in her eyes, and the way her smile lit up the room, it was like she was back with us. My hand instinctively went to cover my eyes, completely overwhelmed with emotions I haven't allowed myself to feel since her passing.

She rushed to me, rubbing my arm, the applause of the room echoed, and I knew I was crying in the middle of this dance. But the care and affection Ginger showed with something like this–by all that she's done since arriving–my hardened shell could no longer deny how sad and grateful I was for this. *I needed this.* I needed this so desperately–to remember the happiness and good of my mother, rather than be so stuck in this dark place I thought was the only way through the grief. And Ginger did it all, without ever knowing my mom personally, and I could collapse from the weight of support, and bond I felt again to my mom. A bond I was afraid was long gone.

Wrapping my arms around her, I hugged her a moment until the tears finally stopped, all the while Ginger whispering reassuringly, "It's okay, let it out" and "I love you, too." When I gathered myself and let her go, she leaned on her tip-toes to kiss my cheek as I looked at my father. He watched the two of us, his face grave and unreadable. After all Ginger has done, and all his disapproval, I wondered if he would make a scene now or after the ball about Ginger pulling such a stunt. Instead, I watched in shock as he walked fervently towards me and wrapped both Ginger and I in a steadied embrace, and I knew now my mouth was wide open, words unable to come at this reaction.

"Thank you. Thank you, *both*. I am so sorry for my behavior these last weeks. You two have made this the best Christmas since your mother passed, and she would be so honored and so proud to see all of what you've created. This portrait is the single greatest thing I've ever seen, other than when Colby was born. Thank you...thank you..."

His last words faded into near sobs and for the first time in years, I hugged my dad like I did as a child. Clinging to him, rubbing his back, burying my face into his neck, I cried along with him. Ginger patted us both, and when we were done, my dad and I wiped our faces as discreetly as we could, adjusting our jackets at the same time, Ginger folded her arms and laughed. "You two are more alike than you think."

Gathering my haughty attitude again, I shook my head and looked at my dad in retaliation.

"I have no idea how you could say such an awful thing, Ginger. Really, I'm much more put together than him, and much less grumpy."

This time, Ginger laughed loudly and unapologetically.

"Less grumpy? Colby, your dad may have been a little apprehensive since I've arrived, but you have been downright the biggest Grinch of all!"

My dad laughed heartily and my spirits lifted. I don't remember the last time I saw him laughing, and now I had more to thank this beautifully annoying Elf. She is opening the door to my father and I mending our relationship, and I longed for that more than I originally thought.

"You Ginger, are a keeper." My dad kissed her cheek and gave me a good slap on the back before walking off to chat with more patrons and guests. I could still hear his laughter in the distance over a joke at a nearby table.

Oh, mom, would you have guessed it'd turn out like this?

I turned my attention back to Ginger, who was watching me intently.

"This portrait of my mom is phenomenal. Who painted it?"

Ginger covered her mouth to hide her words, but she glanced over to the buffet table, her eyes landing on Izabelle who was serving plates to guests.

"She didn't want to publicly take the credit, but I have discovered since our arrival here that Izabelle is one of the best painters I've ever known. A real artist."

Izabelle looked up and met my gaze. I gave a small salute, making her blush before nodding in return.

Ginger came closer again, holding out a hand to me. I took it, pressed a kiss to her fingers, and before I knew it, she was pulling me once again to the dance floor. We spun in a delirium of laughter, making fun of the other's dance moves as the music turned to jazzy Christmas renditions.

Nothing could be better than this.

21

When the Music Fades

Ginger

A s the night drew longer, the closer it was to also getting the last moments I will have with Colby.

For the majority of the evening, I'd done everything I could to put that reminder out of my mind. We danced until our feet were tender, eaten an assortment of the food I prepared, chatted with not only Izabelle, but also with Mr. Jackson—whose entire temperament has gone from blizzard cold to downright warm hearth. There was nothing about this night that wasn't perfect in every way. Every time Colby pulled me by the waist for a kiss, each time he was across the room and his eyes still lingered on mine, all the ways he whispered the most passionate and loving phrases I dared not dream of hearing before—all of it was on the precipice of that same cliff I fell from before, and inching closer to toppling towards the deep unknown.

Unknown to him. Forever known by me.

At any moment, as the night continues to dwindle to soft spoken goodbyes and thank yous, the pitter patter of waiters cleaning up plates, and the final notes of the live music, my sister would be coming to erase Colby's memory of our time together this last month. Then I would know the fate of our triumph or failure here in Everly Cove, if we were able to successfully bring Christmas Spirit levels up enough for Santa to take his ride late tonight—or if Christmas wouldn't come when children across the globe wake tomorrow.

I looked longingly at Colby as he wrapped an arm around his father's shoulder, the two of them talking so amiably, it looked as though they were beginning to go back to the way they used to be—close, happy, and understanding each other and how they individually handled the passing of Everly. It was truly such a blessing to witness them together this way, knowing the hardship they've both endured and the distance that crept between them over the years due to the pain and loss. Now they were clinking a final toast, and as Colby looked my way once more mouthed the words "I love you, Cupcake," I held my tears in place, returning the words that now made my heart break upon exiting my lips.

For this would be the final time I'd ever be able to say them.

The moment Colby's attention returned to his father, I gathered my dress and quietly made my way out of the auditorium, I entered, and found myself on the atrium balcony. Going through the large door at the back of the hallway from the stairwell that led outside, I take final look down at Colby; looking at the man I fell so fast for, but wouldn't find myself letting go of anytime soon, before opening the door and walking onto a long veranda on the back side of the town hall.

Snow was already falling in swirls and dance-like formations around me. I inspected one particular snowflake that caught my eye, its delicate pattern a mix between soft and sharp edges, the tips of each spreading into stars, resembling the top of a Christmas tree. The snowflake fell into my hair, and at last, when it melted away nothing more than a darkened sliver of my red locks, I let the tears go.

"I don't even know what I'm doing here..."

The tears fell harder as I whispered the words to myself. My words turned to puffs of air from the sheer cold, the snow came down harder with each passing minute, but I didn't care. I couldn't bring myself to move, nor bring myself to say a last goodbye to Colby. I couldn't face him when I knew he would soon look upon my face and see only a *stranger*.

Not being there was better for all, but more importantly, it seemed to be the less heartbreaking option for me. I couldn't live with seeing the look of recognition fade from his eyes right before me.

I nearly jumped out of my skin when I heard a sigh from behind me, taking me out of my spiraling thoughts.

Spinning around, my sister stood by the doorway, having opened and closed it without a single sound–or perhaps I was crying so hard I couldn't hear her over my muffled sobs. She didn't look at me, only walked slowly to my side, propping her arms on the balcony railing, looking out into the snowy landscape in front of us.

The sky was quite dark now, but the light coming from the walls behind us illuminated the falling snowflakes, casting shadows in the distance where the lighthouse stood like a beacon of hope, its light waxing and waning as it spun out to give guidance to any nearby boat. But this was no beacon of hope for me; it was merely a cruel reminder of what I've come to love here in Everly Cove, and the reminder that this life was not meant for me.

The silence between my sister and I dragged on, until she eventually spoke softly, almost inaudibly.

"I know why you're here, Ginger...You're here because you love him. And I know seeing his memory erased is something you can't bear to witness."

She was right, as always. If I wasn't so sad, I'd be angry for her taking even more of an opportunity to state the obvious in a moment I was already dreading. But I had no strength for retorts or fighting her words, she was correct. She found me fleeing from the pain I was sure to see—because I was a coward, and couldn't bring myself to say a final goodbye to the man I loved—even if I was never supposed to fall in love with him in the first place.

Clara turned towards me, and I lifted my head, ready for whatever she had to say. Bracing myself for the impact of the words, "It's time." Her green eyes that matched my own, looked at me with a sadness I couldn't place. Clara looked uncomfortable—awkward was actually a better way to describe it. She flexed her hands open several times at her waist, as if she were unsure what to do with them. Unexpectedly, she pulled me hard into her arms and hugged me like she's never hugged me before.

I thought momentarily to push her away, seeing as though a hug from my sister has never been a comfort to me before. But my heart was breaking open into a million shattered icicles, and all

I could do was wrap my arms around her torso and squeeze for all it was worth. Just like our mother did when we were little, she shushed me softly while brushing a hand down my hair, the soothing way she used to when we were so much smaller and so much less controlled by legacy and responsibility. There was a time when we were inseparable, and yet when Elf customs deem the eldest sibling as the bearer of the responsibility of the family's next years, Clara turned rigid and steadfast in her duties, and therefore playtime and sisterly affection became very low on the totem pole.

Still, it felt as it always did before. Before we had to grow up and begin journeys that were expected of us. The North Pole was deeply rooted in tradition, and traditions weren't broken. They were sealed with iron and shut tight. I wondered deep down if she wished for the chains to be looser as well–who knows what she would've done if Elves were able to switch departments and careers? Would she have explored another passion I was unaware of? Would she be lighter, freer, more herself? Were we both just crippled little Elves doing our duty, doing what we could for our family, and yet neglecting us until it became too late? Perhaps that was the true curse of the life of an Elf. The freedom and love I felt being among humans this Christmas–the desire to be able to explore the depths of all you were, not just a small portion as we must adhere to in the Pole–was a cleansing I desperately cherished during my mission here.

So I hugged Clara tighter, hugged her and spoke without words. I hugged her as a thank you, as a way to say I was sorry for all my clumsiness these last years, all the headaches I surely caused as she navigated higher departmental crises and the mounting expectation from our parents to be the best agent she could be. I hugged her until she too, began crying, and we remained in this embrace until my arms ached from how hard I squeezed. When our eyes met, she wiped the tears rolling down my cheek.

"Ginger, I'm so sorry for coming here, interfering with your methods, spying on you, and forcing the protocol in such an impish way. I was actually jealous of your success during your mission."

I blinked several times in confusion.

"*You*? Jealous of *me*?

Clara continued to play with one of my curls in such a sisterly way; although I wasn't used to it anymore, it indeed brought a sense of calm.

"Yes. Out of all the years I've been in the Santa's Helpers department, I've struggled every step of the way. Even though my missions were successful, the promotions have become so consuming, I feel like I can barely keep my Elf feet on the ground. The pressure was always so burdensome, and when you got handed the biggest case in our history, and hearing back from your letter and from Izabelle's at how well you've been doing here–it being your first mission—I admit, I turned a bit green from envy at how seamless your operation was going. And when I found out about you and Colby, I became overwhelmed with this sense that I'd never allowed myself time to find love, to find someone I could confide in, and be comforted by. My life was turned into only work, and seeing you finding a way to raise Spirit levels here, and find somebody you truly cared for...it was as infuriating as it was inspiring. I have longed for more than what I've been living for far longer than I care to admit."

Of all the things my sister could've said, this was the last thing I thought possible to come out of her mouth. We have always had such an epic rivalry, always fussing with each other for attention, accolades, and even the last sugar cookie after supper.

Biting my lip, not sure how to process the new information, I grabbed her hand again.

"All this time, and you've felt the same enormous pressure as I have. The legacy of Tinsels, the success of the missions, the longing for something else. Oh, Clara...I'm so sorry. You are the big sister and the first shoulders our parents propped a mountain on top of. You've had to endure more than I can previously say I was sympathetic about. I wish I could've been there for you more, to help you with all this weight."

Clara quickly wiped at her eye, her nose turning a bright red as she sniffled, doing her best to hold back emotions she'd probably clung to for years.

"You don't need to apologize. *I do*. I'm the big sister, I should've been more supportive. I should've been there for you, to help you in the department rather than leaving you all by yourself. I wish I'd also been able to shut off *"work me"* from *"sister me."* You deserve your big sister again, and you also deserve to hear how incredibly proud I am of you. What you've accomplished here—it will go down in our history books, Ginger."

As she spoke those final words, I was shaken to my core. She smiled at me so brightly, I knew this was the day I've longed for—images of us playing in the snow outside our cottage home in the Pole, decorating gingerbread houses, and holding each other when our first crushes broke our hearts, filled my head like montage of the best movie I'd ever seen.

I couldn't contain myself any longer and hugged Clara as hard as I could. She coughed, patting my back frantically, gasping for air when I released her.

"I definitely forgot how hard of a hugger you were!"

I rolled my eyes at her, looked upwards, holding my arms in the sky like I did when I was young, trying to catch the snowflakes falling like dazzling starlight around me. Clara laughed to herself before raising one hand in the sky, and with a flicker of her fingertips, the snowflakes turned multi-color. Rainbow flecks fell around us, and I spun in circles, allowing the moment of peace to fully encapsulate me. Clara watched as I shot a spark of my magic upwards, causing an array of the crystals to explode like miniature fireworks. When the last of the display dissipated, I faced my sister and shrugged.

"I guess that's it then, we just check the Spiritometer–and hope for the best, right?"

Suddenly, Clara's face soured, her eyes darting towards the doorway leading back to the atrium. With a tremendous exhale, the cheery attitude she had seconds before, evaporated in the cold air surrounding us.

"Well...not quite *it*."

Oh, no...I forgot.

Colby.

22

No Magic Needed, Just Hearts

Colby

"Y ou'll make sure to bring Ginger tomorrow evening for our Christmas dinner, won't you, son?"

My dad shined the grandest smile at me, shaking my hand generously.

"Yes, absolutely. As long as you don't mind having her."

He scoffed like it wasn't just days ago he'd done his utmost to get me back with my ex-girlfriend and belittled the woman I love right in front of me.

Strange how so much can change when one's heart finally reopens.

"Mind? Colby, she is the single greatest thing that's happened to you. I see the two of you together, and you were meant to be. It reminds me of how I felt and looked upon your mother. Ginger is a part of this family now, I wouldn't have it any other way than for her to be with us Christmas night."

With a last wink, he released my hand and left the auditorium, his suit jacket slung over his shoulders like he couldn't believe the events of the evening either. Rubbing the back of my neck in disbelief, I turned to find those hazel eyes that captured my heart.

Instead, all I saw were the last few patrons and waiters finishing cleaning up. My eyes darted around the room searching for Ginger, but in the end, she was nowhere to be found. I saw Izabelle, who was packing a large cake box with the remainder of one of the maple pies Ginger made, which was the best pie of my life, and I rushed to Izabelle's side. When she saw me, she raised an eyebrow at me.

"Hey, you good there?"

Standing beside Izabelle, I continued to purvey the room, and with each passing second my anxiety rose.

It's probably fine, she's most likely in the restroom or something...

"Uh, I think so. Have you seen Ginger recently?"

I was expecting her to say something along the lines of, "Oh, she's right over there," or "She was just saying bye to a few of the attendees." In place of all the sweetly concocted responses I prepared myself for, Izabelle looked around and sighed so hard, I almost couldn't tell if it was annoyance or reluctancy.

Reluctancy for what, though?

Furrowing my brows at her, my anxiety spiked, and I shoved my hands inside my pocket to keep myself occupied.

"Izabelle, what is it? What do you know?"

She pushed the cake box away from her and folded her arms across her chest.

"I really wish I wasn't the one to have to tell you. But seeing that Ginger isn't around, I fear there is no other way. I think she left."

Now my heart thudded in protest in my chest.

"Left? Why would she leave??"

Izabelle walked closer, keeping her voice low, like she was revealing a massive inside job I was unaware of.

"She left because she couldn't bear to watch you forget her."

"Forget her? Izabelle, what the hell are you talking about? How could I ever forge—"

She shushed me and rolled her eyes. Clearly, I was incredibly tiresome for her right now, but for me...it felt like the dream I'd been living in this evening was broken into pieces, and by God I was going to find out why.

"If you let me finish! There is a North Pole protocol, you know how Ginger isn't supposed to expose herself to humans, right?"

She paused, looking at me like each passing moment in my presence was irksome.

"I'm an Elf too, if you didn't get the picture."

"I wouldn't have been able to picture it if I tried...trust me. But Ginger told me right after I found out about her."

"Then you know how serious this is?"

"Not really, she told me about it, but I think there was something she didn't want to mention. It always looked like she was nervous to go into more detail, but I figured it was classified information."

"You're right, there is more. Within that protocol is a procedure in case the incident of exposure gets out. The procedure requires the human to have their memory erased."

"My memory?! And Ginger knew about this?"

"I actually just found out myself...She thought that if she was successful in her mission to raise Spirit levels in Everly Cove, she might be able to plead her case about you and your involvement, how much you helped during her time here, and could ask for them to spare your memory. But last night, her older sister showed up; she's a manager in the department, and she told Ginger the protocol would happen tonight, as the ball came to an end, to give you both your last moments together."

Shaking my head, I felt it spin from the weight of the information.

"So the protocol wouldn't just erase my memory of Ginger being an Elf, it would erase her altogether?"

When Izabelle didn't answer, I knew my assumption was correct. I was nervous about what would happen once Christmas was over, but I imagined it'd be more like a difficult long-distance relationship...not a relationship that I wouldn't know ever happened! Not a relationship I wanted so much now, my life forever altered by those adorable pointed ears and kind heart that saved me this Christmas.

"Izabelle, we have to find her. There's no way I am going to let her leave me this way. No way I am going to let her go."

Desperation laced my words, and I knew I was sounding ridiculous–how can one human guy fend off all of the hundreds of years of tradition and procedures of The North Pole in one month? In one night? There was no guarantee I'd find Ginger before her sister erased my memory, but if I had to borrow a reindeer from the zoo and ask Izabelle to sprinkle her magic on it to get me there…I'll do it.

Izabelle smiled in a way that showed she understood, and she wouldn't let me lose Ginger.

"Agreed, and I know she only left to protect her heart because she loves you so much."

"And I really love her, too. More than I've ever loved another person."

"But have you ever noticed how stubborn that girl is?"

"Oh, yeah, she's the most stubborn person I've ever met. I love her for it."

"She really needs to understand that her friends are by her side, even when the going gets rough."

I covered my mouth to feign shock.

"Izabelle! Who knew you were such a romantic?"

She blushed, throwing her hands in the air in acceptance.

"Yeah, yeah…don't tell anyone. But Ginger and I have grown so close since coming here, and she really is one of the best people I've ever met. There's no way I'd ruin her happiness, even though in my opinion, you are a bit too smug for your own good sometimes."

"You have such a way with words! Stop trying to flatter me, I'm a taken man. Now will you help me find her?"

She puffed in frustration.

"Do you ever get over yourself, even when time is literally ticking away?"

"Where's the fun in that?"

Izabelle smiled faintly and shook her head at me, deliberately ignoring my question. For the first time in minutes, the slight panic that spread throughout my veins vanished.

Gathering a small phone device, I believe is the Spiritometer like Ginger's I've seen briefly, she clicked several buttons on it before shouting out a triumphant "A-ha!"

"I can track her Spiritometer. She's still here in the town hall–come with me!"

Izabelle grabbed the bottom of her black gown and lifted it up, kicked off her heels in one fluid motion, and without waiting for me to respond, sprinted towards the spiral staircase and up to the atrium. My years of hockey back in high school and how fast I needed to kick off the ice for drills were finally coming back in handy. Running as fast as I could, I followed Izabelle upstairs and out the door leading to the balcony. I sighed in relief when Ginger's eyes blinked in confusion as we saw each other.

We still have time.

Huffing wildly to catch my breath, I strode toward her without saying a word and pulled her by the wrists to collapse into my arms. Wrapped around her waist, the hopelessness I felt when Izabelle told me she was leaving, fully unraveled as I hugged her tight.

Because in reality, I've realized it did. She brought me home, made me see I was more than my father or anyone else's expectations, showed me I was loveable for exactly who I am, not some version of myself another wished to create. Her sweet voice melted my heart as she spoke against my chest, her fists clenching the back of my jacket.

"Colby, you're here...you found me."

I moved back enough to firmly hold her chin, forcing her to look up at me. My voice eased into the one I always spoke with her, a gentility I didn't know I was capable of before. Because despite it feeling like she took my heart and ripped it from my ribcage by trying to leave before I knew why–*or could remember why*–I couldn't be angry with her. If the situations were reversed and I knew in a matter of moments she'd forget everything about me, I know I wouldn't be able to handle seeing it happen either. I whispered so only she could hear me, needing her to hear my desperation, my temporary heartache.

"Cupcake, you can't think for a second I'm letting you go that easily."

Her eyes swam with the desire I also wished to take from words to actions. Still clinging to me, she scans my face like she wasn't sure she'd ever see it again.

"I'm so sorry I left, I couldn't imagine watching as you forgot me."

Brushing the strand of hair that always fell in her face, I plastered on my nonchalant attitude and smirked at her as if what she was saying was the craziest thing I've heard all year, which other than finding out Elves and Santa exist, *this was.*

"Forget you? Ginger, it'd take an army of Elves with dozens of memory eraser thingies to make me forget you. And even then, I know I'd find a way back to you. There's no coming back from dreaming of you by my side."

Izabelle coughed and looked away, muttering something beneath her breath.

"Actually, it only takes one memory device to erase everything, but..."

I glared at Ginger's now-permanent, overly sarcastic friend over Ginger's shoulder.

"Come on, Bells. You're ruining a very romantic moment here."

She put a hand on her hip and gave me a death glare.

"Call me Bells again, and I'll personally see to it that you lose the memory of what a big head you have, Colby Jackson."

Ginger laughed loudly, and the sound reassured me, even though the danger was still present. Returning my attention to Ginger, I yelled back towards Izabelle, swatting the air as if I was shooing her away.

"Love ya, too, you soft-hearted meanie."

Another cough drew my attention towards the balcony, where an almost identical woman sporting Ginger's red locks stood. She looked so similar to Ginger, but her hair was straighter, her eyes less joyful and she had a look on her face like the scene playing out before her was too cutesy for her and she didn't know where to look or what to do.

She stepped towards Ginger, and I brought Ginger a little closer to me again.

"Hi, Colby. I'm Clara, Ginger's sister."

I tucked Ginger under my arm, refusing to let her out of my grip, protectively holding her waist.

"I've heard about you. I've heard you came to erase my memory."

Ginger's head dropped, and she wiped under her eyes, already crying at what was about to happen. I continued to stand my ground; she may be Ginger's sister, but she didn't know how hard a fight I'd go through for her.

"You heard correctly...I have come here to erase your memory...But I can't do it. I won't do that to my sister."

My mouth dropped open, and Ginger gasped beside me, clearly just as surprised by the change of heart. Of all the discussions we've had together about Clara, about how hard she was to deal with, about the way she scolded Ginger, and always did everything by the rulebook–this had to be some sort of trick. Ginger had the same thought as I did.

"You're not going to do it?? What do you mean? You said it was the only way, and we don't even know if we succeeded in saving Christmas. How are you not going to enact the protocol, especially if I've failed here?"

Clara lifted her own Spiritometer out of her pant pocket, the screen illuminating her stern face in the darkness of the night. She turned the screen facing us, handing it to Ginger.

"Take a look."

Ginger hesitated, looking up at me, before grabbing the Spiritometer and taking a look at the screen. Before I knew it, she was jumping around beside me, shouting.

"We did it!! Colby! Izabelle! We saved Christmas!"

Izabelle rushed over and took the device from Ginger's hand, inspecting it before she laughed out loud.

"I can't believe it! This will go down in Elf history!"

Both Izabelle and Ginger began jumping up and down, while Clara smiled broadly as I stood in amazement at the fact Izabelle was squealing like a child alongside Ginger. When Izabelle caught my eye and a flare of embarrassment lit her face, I winked at her and she shrugged, continuing to hug Ginger back as she jumped like Zeus always does when he's over-excited.

Clara made her way closer to me and cleared her throat.

"I'm sorry we had to meet under such circumstances. I'm glad my sister has you."

Eyeing her, I patted her back like we were old friends who just had a misunderstanding.

"Don't worry about it, I'm glad she has a sister like you looking out for her."

Clara smiled, watching the others spin around.

"I've already sent correspondence to Headquarters; I'm not really sure what will happen, but I have shown my support for your relationship together, and I believe they will hear us out, considering the success this mission was and the role you played in it. I plan to make a full report in person tomorrow on your behalf."

"Thank you, so much. It means the world to me you'd do that for us. If you don't have to rush off too fast, would you like to stay and have Christmas dinner with us tomorrow?"

Clara's eyebrows shot up in surprise, thinking for a moment, and looked between Ginger and me.

"I'd love to, count me in!"

At Clara's acceptance, we stood silently again as I looked back to Ginger, who was giggling and throwing her hands in the air, her magic shooting out in red and green sparks in celebration. Without another second to lose, I bolted across the veranda and scooped Ginger into my arms, raising her up with her feet dangling. She cupped my face and smashed her lips against mine, our tongues intertwining in a flurry of frenzied emotions. I kept kissing her without a care in the world, pouring, with all my heart, into each motion of our lips.

Because for right now, she wasn't going anywhere but back home with me, to remind her just how much I love her, in every possible way. Fall asleep in my arms the way she was supposed to, and wake up to the first Christmas in years where I actually looked forward to.

23

A Recipe to Forever

Ginger

*O**ne Month Later*

"Alright, you blasted thing. You will NOT best me. Do you hear me?"

I stepped back and waited in anticipation. After several agonizing seconds, the espresso machine at last began pouring and I let go of the breath I was holding.

"Ha! Even after all this time, you can't beat me."

A chuckle came from behind me from where Colby walked out of the café kitchen holding a box of cookware.

"Are you getting your butt handed to you again by that machine, Cupcake?"

"No! I'm winning, as always. But it still gives me such an attitude."

Colby set the box down on an empty table, walking to wrap his arms around my waist, pulling my hair back to kiss along my neck, his words were muffled against my skin as I bit my lip at the sensation of his breath on me.

"It only gives you attitude because you've got to be gentle with it."

Smiling, he turns me around, I lift on my tip-toes for a kiss. I speak against his mouth in between kisses.

"Mhm, gentle. You'll have to remind me of how good at being gentle you can be as a refresher."

Colby moaned into my mouth, his hands squeezing my butt in response, until he gave me a small smack and brought me back down to the floor.

"When we get to our apartment in New York, I guarantee a demonstration. But you, Cupcake, need to finish packing like...yesterday."

It was true, I was behind on packing to leave for New York, but there was so much to get settled before our departure. I needed to make sure everything was just right so that the café would continue to succeed after we left. Taking me out of my thoughts, Izabelle sauntered in from the front door with another box of items, Gimli and Zeus following behind her.

Zeus came sprinting toward Colby, who rubbed his ears, Gimli meowing an incredibly kind remark.

"Thank you Gimli, it's okay. I'm only a little sad about leaving."

Izabelle placed the box on the floor and cracked her back. She'd been helping me get things together all week—she was *the* best friend!

"You act like you'll never come back here! Even though you're going to New York for Colby's culinary school and your new bakery to replicate what you did here, doesn't mean you won't be coming back. As the new Human—Elf Coordinator, you'll be coming back every few months to check on progress in Everly Cove and the café now that we have a permanent collection of both human and Elf employees here."

She wasn't wrong. This past Christmas has changed everything for not only me, but for the North Pole. The day after Christmas dinner was spent with Colby, his father and aunt, Izabelle and even my own sister, where we ate the best food, played Christmas trivia, and even exchanged gifts–I was currently spotting mine: a gorgeous snowflake necklace that changed colors depending on my mood, gifted by Colby. The following morning, my sister departed to the North Pole to speak on our behalf, and we waited a grueling 3 days before hearing a response from her. When her letter arrived, Izabelle, Colby, and myself argued for 10 mins over who should open it, until finally Izabelle scolded us both and did it so fast, we didn't even have time to stop her.

That letter changed everything. Our case was accepted, and beyond that, Colby got to keep his memory, the North Pole having realized the benefit of implementing humans into our world. News of the festival's success spread quickly: Colby and countless others had not only saved Everly Cove but raised Christmas Spirit to 115%—a level unseen in over a hundred years. When Santa heard, he wasted no time. Summoning Elves from every department, he announced a bold new plan: humans would now be hired to serve at the North Pole and at agency branches across the globe.

And I was named the leader of it! That's right, Ginger Tinsel was now the head of the Human–Elf Recruitment Department. Or as I have had fun calling it, Ginger's Merry Mates! The nickname wasn't catching on yet, but who's to say it wouldn't?

The very same day, the acceptance letter to the Culinary School of America in New York came after Colby's friend Tom secretly mailed it on his behalf. I'd never seen Colby so excited, and when he shyly produced the letter to his father, he was greeted with the biggest hug and congratulations. Many tears were shed as his father said he only wanted what was best for him, and Everly Cove would always be his home, whether he was mayor or not.

Ever since, Colby and I have been in deep preparation mode as we decided to move together to New York so he could pursue school and I...a bakery all on my own while there. I could make it whatever I wished, and it wouldn't interfere with running the human recruitment. I also specifically chose to set up Everly Cove as our new Merry Mates headquarters. After all, it is the beloved town that gave us our start!

The plan was set: every few months, department recruits would gather in Everly Cove to review events and missions. From there, agents would be sent across the world to continue recruiting humans, bringing them into our world to help maintain Spirit levels and to learn from one another—just as I had learned from the people of Everly Cove.

While I ran this department, I was being allowed by the Pole to open my very own bakery. One that was all mine, all my creations, one I could explore the depths of my love for sweet treats and goodies that brought people together. My dream was coming true, in more ways than one, and it was all because they took a chance on this clumsy Elf. Not to mention, everyone in Everly Cove, especially Colby, reminded me what was important: *to never give up on those you care for, or yourself.*

I looked between Izabelle and Colby and smiled brightly.

"You're right, Izabelle, we will be back."

Colby stood beside me, wrapping his arm over my shoulder.

"It's time to go, are you ready?"

Looking around the café, I take in the cozy space that housed me when I was a scared Elf on a mission she wasn't sure would succeed. The place that held so many kind faces that welcomed me like one of their own. The place I first started falling in love with Colby. Nodding, I nudged him in the ribs playfully.

"More than ready!"

Gimli and Zeus bounded together towards the door, Izabelle carried out the box she'd brought after shoving her pocket full with a few last-minute cookies I'd made, and Colby winked at me before following behind her. As I stood at the doorway, I took a final glance back, thinking about how this Christmas showed me that dreams could be made real, even if they didn't happen at all how you expected.

But perhaps that's the joy of Christmas, that wishes can be made even better than you dreamt. How do the children of the world come to enjoy the magic of Christmas so much? They do it with an open heart, wishes upon stars, and the hope that no matter what, tomorrow we can try to keep working towards a better and brighter world.

Maybe that was the ultimate gift of Christmas: *to believe*. To believe that we all deserve good things, good people in our lives, and that perhaps...the world isn't so Elfed up after all.

Although, I gave it a good attempt, didn't I?